Music Washed Over Him, Ebbing And Flowing Like The Tide.

As the piano fell silent, one note lingering in the night, Devlin knew he'd been given a rare insight into the heart of Kathleen Moira Gallagher, agent of the Black Watch, now simply a grieving woman whose soul stumbled.

When he had followed her to Summer Island, it was to quiet a need he thought had died forever. To subdue a faltering, resurrected impulse to ease the hurts of others, to make himself believe that he could lead her back to the life she should have.

And without intending it, he'd found himself on this part of the shore, sitting at the base of zigzagging steps leading where he'd never meant to go.

To Kate...

Dear Reader,

This April of our 20th anniversary year, Silhouette will continue to shower you with powerful, passionate, provocative love stories!

Cait London offers an irresistible MAN OF THE MONTH, *Last Dance,* which also launches her brand-new miniseries FREEDOM VALLEY. Sparks fly when a strong woman tries to fight her feelings for the rugged man who's returned from her past. *Night Music* is another winner from BJ James's popular BLACK WATCH series. Read this touching story about two wounded souls who find redeeming love in each other's arms.

Anne Marie Winston returns to Desire with her emotionally provocative *Seduction, Cowboy Style,* about an alpha male cowboy who seeks revenge by seducing his enemy's sister. In *The Barons of Texas: Jill* by Fayrene Preston, THE BARONS OF TEXAS miniseries offers another feisty sister, and the sexy Texan who claims her.

Desire's theme promotion THE BABY BANK, in which interesting events occur on the way to the sperm bank, continues with Katherine Garbera's *Her Baby's Father.* And Barbara McCauley's scandalously sexy miniseries SECRETS! offers another tantalizing tale with *Callan's Proposition,* featuring a boss who masquerades as his secretary's fiancé.

Please join in the celebration of Silhouette's 20th anniversary by indulging in all six Desire titles—which will fulfill *your* every desire!

Enjoy!

Joan Marlow Golan

Joan Marlow Golan
Senior Editor, Silhouette Desire

Please address questions and book requests to:
Silhouette Reader Service
U.S.: 3010 Walden Ave., P.O. Box 1325, Buffalo, NY 14269
Canadian: P.O. Box 609, Fort Erie, Ont. L2A 5X3

Night Music

BJ JAMES

Silhouette® Desire

Published by Silhouette Books

America's Publisher of Contemporary Romance

SILHOUETTE BOOKS

ISBN 0-373-76286-0

NIGHT MUSIC

Copyright © 2000 by BJ James

This edition published by arrangement with Harlequin Books S.A.

® and TM are trademarks of Harlequin Books S.A., used under license.
Trademarks indicated with ® are registered in the United States Patent
and Trademark Office, the Canadian Trade Marks Office and in other
countries.

Visit Silhouette at www.eHarlequin.com

Printed in U.S.A.

Books by BJ James

BJ JAMES

married her high school sweetheart straight out of college and soon found that books were delightful companions during her lonely nights as a doctor's wife. But she never dreamed she'd be more than a reader, never expected to be one of the blessed, letting her imagination soar, weaving magic of her own.

BJ has twice been honored by the Georgia Romance Writers with their prestigious Maggie Award for Best Short Contemporary Romance. She has also received the following awards from *Romantic Times Magazine*: Critic's Choice Award of 1994-1995, Career Achievement Award for Series Storyteller of the Year and Best Desire of 1994-1995 for *The Saint of Bourbon Street*.

IT'S OUR 20th ANNIVERSARY!
We'll be celebrating all year,
Continuing with these fabulous titles,
On sale in April 2000.

Romance

#1438 Carried Away
Kasey Michaels/Joan Hohl

#1439 An Eligible Stranger
Tracy Sinclair

#1440 A Royal Marriage
Cara Colter

#1441 His Wild Young Bride
Donna Clayton

#1442 At the Billionaire's Bidding
Myrna Mackenzie

#1443 The Marriage Badge
Sharon De Vita

Desire

#1285 Last Dance
Cait London

#1286 Night Music
BJ James

#1287 Seduction, Cowboy Style
Anne Marie Winston

#1288 The Barons of Texas: Jill
Fayrene Preston

#1289 Her Baby's Father
Katherine Garbera

SECRETS! #1290 Callan's Proposition
Barbara McCauley

Intimate Moments

#997 The Wildes of Wyoming—Hazard
Ruth Langan

#998 Daddy by Choice
Paula Detmer Riggs

#999 The Harder They Fall
Merline Lovelace

#1000 Angel Meets the Badman
Maggie Shayne

#1001 Cinderella and the Spy
Sally Tyler Hayes

#1002 Safe in His Arms
Christine Scott

Special Edition

#1315 Beginning with Baby
Christie Ridgway

#1316 The Sheik's Kidnapped Bride
Susan Mallery

#1317 Make Way for Babies!
Laurie Paige

#1318 Surprise Partners
Gina Wilkins

#1319 Her Wildest Wedding Dreams
Celeste Hamilton

#1320 Soul Mates
Carol Finch

Foreword

In desperate answer to a need prompted by changing times and mores, Simon McKinzie, dedicated and uncompromising leader of The Black Watch, has been called upon by the president of the United States to form a more covert and more dangerous division of his most clandestine clan. Ranging the world in ongoing assembly of this unique unit, he has gathered and will gather in the elite among the elite—those born with the gift or the curse of skills transcending the norm. Men and women who bring extraordinary and uncommon talents in answer to extraordinary and uncommon demands. They are, in most cases, men and women who have plummeted to the brink of hell because of their talents. Tortured souls who have stared down into the maw of destruction, been burned by its fires, yet have come back, better, surer, stronger. Driven and colder.

As officially nameless as The Black Watch, to those few who have had misfortune and need of calling on their dark service, they are known as Simon's chosen... Simon's Marauders.

Prologue

Out of the dawn a screaming wind snaked over frigid mountain slopes. A faceless, formless leviathan hurling snow and ice with the force to flay skin and flesh to the bone.

A killing madness.

Death, dressed in white.

Within a bulwark of twisted metal and scorched canvas, sheltered by ramparts of boulders, a man and a woman lay prone, bodies entwined. She was fragile. Her hair, a mass of auburn falling from a knitted cap, trailed over his arm to mingle like fire into ice. He was lean and rugged, his skin darkened by wind and weather. His hair, thick and close-cut, was as black as snow was white.

Holding her, offering what warmth he could, he whispered to her. His lips moving against bright curls, his breath skimming a waxen cheek. While he soothed her with nonsense and promises, a wall of snow built slowly at their backs. The malicious gift of a monster, bringing a modicum of protection, even as it concealed evidence of the charred, shattered plane, its pilot, and his sole passenger.

Yet, the wall would be one more buffer of hope against the storm. Hope, buying time. Time to survive, perhaps time to die.

She was a stranger to the mountain. Content to stay behind each time a plane lifted off filled with climbers her husband hoped to guide to the summit, she couldn't know the gravity of their situation. For as long as he could keep it that way, she wouldn't. This he'd promised from the first. Not as her pilot, but as a friend.

For three days, he'd kept his promise. He would keep it to the end. As long as there was a shred of hope, she, above all, would cling to the will to live.

"Maybe long enough for a miracle." He didn't realize he'd fallen silent, listening to the wind. Or that he'd spoken again. His voice was rough, but something in it touched a chord.

Rousing, she looked at him through feverish eyes. Struggling to one elbow, she tried to concentrate. "Jock?"

The mistake sent an icy dread through him. Hallucination; she was deteriorating more than he feared. But he wouldn't give up hope. Not yet. "Shh." With the back of a hand whitened by cold he traced the curve of her cheek. "We'll talk when the storm calms."

As if she didn't hear him, catching his hand, turning his palm to her glazed gaze, she whispered, "You're hurt?"

Realizing she hadn't the breath for more, he assured her. "The burns will heal."

"Burns? How?" The words were a gasp, the effort a struggle.

"Grabbed something hot." Heartened by this lucid perception, as he took back his hand he added in a wry understatement, "Something I knew was hot."

She laughed feebly. A caricature of the sound that brightened the lives of all who knew her. Caressing his face with fingers tipped by nails gone black, she whispered, "My fearless Jock. You never..." Each word was a ragged wheeze as she fought for breaths that never seemed to reach her lungs. Her gaze drifted. As she lost her point of focus, her eyes rolled back, nearly disappearing within their sockets.

"Joy!" Willing her to hear, he muttered, "Tell me." Afraid before if she squandered precious strength to speak, he was more afraid now if she couldn't. While the screech of the wind and a mad flap of canvas quieted, he brushed her cheek with his and kissed her temple as Jock would. "Talk to me, Joy."

With her breathing eased in the lessened force of the wind, a tiny bit of the color returned to her face. Her lips moved, then there were words. "Never..." The chuckle was half cough, yet still her trademark laugh. "Never learn, Jockolove."

"No, Joyful girl." He was Devlin O'Hara, not Jock. But if it would help, he would be the person she desperately needed him to be. Murmuring the endearment he'd heard so many times, he slipped into the role of lover, for a friend. "That's why I need you."

She nodded, her chin resting so long against her chest, he feared she wouldn't lift her head again. Recalling the name that defined her, he prompted softly, "Joyful?"

Lashes fluttering against her cheeks, she tried another laugh. As Joy always laughed, even in the worst of times. "Still here." Her voice grew clearer. A fit of shivering abated, as if her body hadn't the strength for more than one exertion. But when she lifted her gaze there was light, the illumination of a kind soul and happy heart. "Couldn't wait for you to come down the slope. Couldn't wait to tell you.''

"What was so important, sweet Joyful?"

As if it would listen, the wind calmed again, then ceased. From their paltry shelter, he looked on a desert of white. With every jagged pile of stone, every jutting rock obliterated by snow.

Silence, as deep as the peak was tall, crackled in still air. Wrapping her tighter in tattered clothing he'd managed to snatch from the burning plane, he lowered her to a makeshift pallet. With his arms cradling her, he waited.

So long after his question that he thought she'd drifted away, in a voice filled with a wonder, she told a labored story.

He didn't mean to interrupt the broken flow, nor shatter the whispered hope, but once his control slipped. Jerking back, he stared down at her. "God help me! I didn't know."

The palm of her hand folded over his lips, her fingers curled around his chin. "Don't! I know I promised, but the doctor thinks the damage the rheumatic fever…''

As her voice gathered strength, he listened to lilting words grotesquely at odds with the gray cast of her skin and the rattle of each hard-won breath. As mute as stone, as grave, he learned of the risk she'd taken to make this ill-fated flight.

Long after her story was finished, he held her. Long after she slept an unnatural sleep, he watched over her as he had for days. Finally he slept, as well.

When he woke, the day was brighter, impossibly tranquil. His first thought was of Joy. Touching her throat, he checked her pulse. The beat of her heart was erratic. But that it beat at all was cause for celebration.

Stimulated by a surge of adrenaline, an insightful mind

began to function positively. What he'd perceived as the final disaster, he recognized as a final gift of the mountain.

Extracting himself from her embrace, praying one breath would follow another, he waited until a mild restlessness subsided. Reluctant to leave, certain he must if she would have any chance of living out a dream, he turned abruptly. Stepping from their shelter, pausing only to orient himself, he set his plan in motion.

Later, taxed beyond human endurance, with the sweat of his struggle turned to dangerous rime beneath his clothing, he staggered back to shelter. Back to Joy.

She neither woke nor stirred as he gathered her to him. Soon he was as silent, as still.

He didn't wake when the Lama, a high-altitude rescue helicopter, passed over. Nor when it returned to fly so low its blades swept away the message stamped into rare loose snow. He didn't wake when the first of its team reached the shelter. Nor did he hear the jubilant cry, "Survivors. Good God! We have survivors!"

In the midst of the exhilaration of four dedicated men, only a voice he knew and a hand gripping his arm roused him. But as numb senses rallied, eyes burned by glare wouldn't see. "Jock?"

"Yes, Dev."

The familiar voice echoed in the darkness of his mind. "I tried to keep her warm."

"I know." No one among the search team, least of all Jock Bohannon, could believe this man had done as much as he had, as long as he had. The message was a wonder in itself. "Give her to me, Dev. We have to get you out of here."

He pulled away, his befuddled mind clinging doggedly to his one purpose. "I have to take care of Joy."

"You have. Now let me."

"Jock?" Memory sparked, the veil began to lift. "I'm sorry. I didn't know about her heart."

"She didn't want you to. She didn't want anyone to know." Carefully prizing burned, frostbitten hands from their burden, Jock took his wife into his arms. "I'll take care of her now."

"The cold hurts. Don't let her be cold."

"She won't ever be cold again." There were tears on Jock Bohannon's craggy face as he whispered, "I promise."

When the Lama lifted from the mountain, and while the wounded man slept, the rescue team looked down on a pitiful shelter built by horrendously burned hands. Once again, against impossible odds, one of the extraordinary men known as Alaska's Denali fliers had accomplished an incredible feat.

Devlin O'Hara had beaten the mountain. But fate had played the last hand, sending a second freak storm to the lowlands, grounding the Lama's desperate last-ditch search for an hour.

An hour too long, a grieving Jock Bohannon thought as he caressed his wife's still face. An hour too late.

One

"**M**ayday! Mayday! We're going down."

As sweat beaded his forehead and plastered shaggy hair to his rigid throat, Devlin O'Hara shivered. Muscles tensed. Scarred hands curled into fists. "We're breaking up." His tone turned guttural. His body arched, from a straining throat rose a desperate cry. "Fire! We have a fire."

Then the night was still. In utter calm, a waning moon cast pale patterns over a rippled expanse of white. Silence deepened.

Then it began. The shivering, the hushed plea.

"Please." Shivering became shudders. "Oh, God! Too high, too cold." A body honed to muscle and sinew tensed.

"No!" Lurching upright, his eyes flickered open, ending a remembered nightmare. As he stared through the birth of dawn, a frozen mountain slope faded, becoming his childhood bedroom.

Throwing a soaked sheet aside, unmindful of his nakedness, he walked to the open window. Flinging the curtain aside, bathed in the nuance of daybreak, Devlin O'Hara watched as crimson streaked across the horizon, painting the bay in dark fire.

An autumn sunrise over the Chesapeake, one of his favorite memories, in his favorite place, his favorite season.

The house was tranquil, but its dignified repose would be short-lived. His family would be waking with the sun, eager for the adventure of a new day. The joyful adventure of coming together.

In growing numbers, with various names, but O'Haras still, they had come. And, for a while, they would be simply family. Mavis and Keegan asked nothing more of their unique brood than this time.

He hadn't planned this visit. He hadn't planned anything beyond making it through each minute of each day for months. Yet, on the eve of the appointed time, he found himself packing, then taking leave of many friends...and one nemesis.

But now he knew there was no escape. The deadly beauty and tragedy of the mountain went with him wherever he might go. Even here. This sanctuary of sanctuaries was no longer his.

Denali lived in his days and nights. And Joy died.

They always would.

Wearily, Devlin closed the curtain on a new day on the Chesapeake. He didn't deserve this place or this family.

He shouldn't have come.

"So, what do you think?" Leaning against the antique frame of leaded windows, Valentina O'Hara Courtenay stared through polished panes, pondering her own question.

Anyone but an O'Hara would have been awed by the

house and the charm of the view. But to the five siblings gathered for the annual reunion, it was simply home. And, sometimes, sanctuary.

From the look of the man who walked the shore that lay beyond the lawn, it was the latter he needed. If he didn't flee, he would be here two weeks. But could an autumn fortnight spent by the Chesapeake resolve the troubles plaguing Devlin?

"I don't care what he says, he isn't fine," she declared, facing her younger sister. "He's too quiet. Too alone."

"Val, no one walks away from the loss of a friend unscathed," Patience reminded gently. "Five months isn't nearly long enough to console one who cares as deeply as Devlin."

"Of course not," Val conceded. "It's natural he still grieves. But you can't believe that's all it is any more than I do."

"No." Patience sighed. "And it isn't his hands. His next lady love should find the scars interesting more than ugly."

"If there is one," Val drawled as she prowled the room.

"There's always a lady in Devlin's life, Val."

"Precisely." Val leaped on the comment. "Until now."

The point made, both fell silent. Restlessly, Valentina paced, only to pause before a wall of family portraits. Studying each, she named them in order, eldest to youngest. "Look at us. Devlin, Kieran, Tynan, Valentina, Patience, eternally sixteen."

"Only in portraits." Far into her third pregnancy, Patience felt much older than sixteen.

Valentina hardly heard. "No more than a year or two separates either of us from the next. We look and think alike, up to a point. With Devlin as our standard. We wanted to be like him. Beautiful Devlin, of the blackest hair, the bluest eyes."

"Yet it was never as much that he was oldest, or how he looked, as his kindness and caring, and courage." Patience smiled, remembering. "Able to leap tall buildings in a single bound."

"Superman," Valentina agreed fondly. "Bigger than life. His smile quicker, his passion greater, his heart most tender."

"Now he rarely smiles," Patience observed sadly. "If he feels anything, it doesn't show."

"Or the reverse?" Valentina ventured. "Is what he's feeling so awful, he dares not let us see?"

"But we're family, Val. If he's hurting, we can help."

"Can we?" Valentina turned from the window. "Perhaps the mountain took something from him only he can get back."

Patience understood her sister's logic, Devlin's behavior was strange. They were accustomed to his solitary disappearances. But if there was ever trouble, he found a way to communicate, to reassure his family. With the crash, there had been only silence.

Months later, he'd written, saying he wouldn't make the family gathering. Only then had he spoken of the crash and Joy.

Despite their worry about his uncharacteristic behavior, keeping a childhood rule that still guided their lives, no one questioned, no one interfered. No one understood.

Until he'd walked through the door two days before, weary, thin, dreadfully haggard, no one expected to see him. In a way, Patience thought, none of them had. The real Devlin bore little resemblance to the grim specter who haunted the shore.

"He's like a stranger." Devlin had moved from sight, but Valentina knew he hadn't gone far. His reluctance to leave the house and grounds, or to mingle with his own, was patent. "I suspect he feels like a stranger even to himself."

Patience sighed. "I don't understand."

"Hopefully we will soon." Val grimaced. "I broke the rule."

There were few rules within the family, and Patience knew instinctively which her sister had broken. "What have you done?"

"I'm interfering. I called Simon."

Patience nodded. Who else would Val call? Simon McKinzie, commander of The Black Watch and the most powerful man in covert operations, could unearth the problem. "When will you know?"

"He promised by two."

Patience glanced at a clock. "Less than five minutes."

Valentina caught an uneven breath. "Was I wrong? None of us has ever intruded so blatantly before."

"You weren't wrong. Even though he needs someone, Devlin's shut us out. No," Patience repeated firmly. "You weren't wrong."

"He might hate me."

Stretching out her hand, Patience waited until Valentina clasped it in her own. "Devlin could never hate you. He may not be happy with this at first, but in the end, he'll thank you for having the wisdom to know when a rule should be broken. As I do."

In concert, the clock boomed the hour, and within a cabinet housing instruments of modern technology, a fax machine chattered. Both women froze, hands clenched. It was only when the machine fell silent that their fingers drifted apart.

Valentina moved to the cabinet to take out the printed sheet. Turning, she came to Patience and, in deference to the concern she saw on her sister's face, laid the document before her.

Patience read slowly, carefully, with the gleam of tears
in her eyes before she was half through. When she finished, wordlessly, she returned the single sheet to Valentina.

Valentina absorbed each word. Contained here were the
facts that had changed her brother into a man she didn't
know. As Patience had, she read slowly, carefully. Finally,
with a heavy heart, she tucked away the report that
changed all the rules. "I'm not sorry anymore. Now I
know what to do."

"How can I help?"

Valentina's lips lifted in a smile. "You've done enough
by listening and supporting my choice. But there is one
more favor."

"Anything."

"If you would make my excuses, for the rest of the
day."

Patience nodded shrewdly. "You're leaving the island."

"As soon as possible."

"Where will you go?"

With an elegant lift of her shoulders, Valentina asked,
"Where would I go with a problem of this sort?"

"To Simon," Patience supplied softly.

"Good afternoon, Simon."

When the door to his private office opened unannounced,
Simon McKinzie knew who his intruder would be. No one
else among The Black Watch would dare such a bold act.

"Ahh. Mrs. Courtenay, I thought you had retired."
Leaning back in his chair, he glared at her. "What happened to knocking?"

"I have. And what happened to 'Good afternoon'?"

"Perhaps it went the way of knocking before entering."

Valentina had the grace to be truly contrite. "I'm sorry,
but there's a problem only you can help resolve."

Simon took stock. Who among his agents was facing personal problems? Before retiring from The Watch, Valentina had possessed a magical radar when it came to sensing troubles within the organization. "What is it now?" he asked. "Or should I say who?"

"My brother."

"By my count, you have three, missy."

"It's Devlin."

"Devlin isn't one of mine." Though not from lack of trying, Simon admitted. Devlin O'Hara was perfect for The Watch. But beyond the rare assignment, he eluded its persuasive leader.

"He has been, on occasion."

Simon had leaned back until his chair teetered on two legs. Now it banged down. "How the devil could you know that?"

Despite her worry, Val laughed. "Lucky guess."

"Remind me not to play poker with you," he grumbled.

"Consider yourself reminded." Advancing to the desk, she leaned closer. "Will you help?"

"Sorry, missy, that's impossible. In the first place…"

Valentina caught his hand in hers. Folding each finger to form the fist he would have made with each of five points, she held it tightly. Every agent knew the gesture. "Simon, there is no first place, or fifth. This is Devlin, the strongest and best of us."

Simon nodded as she released his fist. "Denali."

Of course he knew. He would have gathered the information himself. "Then you understand the problem."

"I know the facts and ramifications," he corrected. "I'm sure no one understands the problem, or the solution as you do."

"Isn't it obvious?"

"Ahh, in case it isn't, why don't you explain."

"Who is Devlin?" She asked. "What is he to us?"

"Your brother, your hero and knight gallant." Simon knew the direction she was taking this. But it would be interesting to see how far she would go.

"For as long as we can remember, there's always been someone he could rescue, or care for, or protect. Now he believes he failed on Denali. As long as he does, he'll never forgive himself."

"So you would offer him a chance to redeem himself," Simon suggested. "Hoping in redemption, he finds forgiveness."

"That's where you come in. He needs a damsel in distress."

"One of my damsels." Simon didn't wait for an answer. "And no doubt you know exactly who."

"Exactly. With your permission, of course."

"Of course." He watched her for a considering moment. "Does this damsel have a name?"

"Kate Gallagher."

"What do you know about Kate, missy?"

"I met her once, outside your office."

"Once?" Simon lifted a shaggy brow. "From that, you deduce she's what your brother needs?"

Valentina didn't hesitate. "I liked what I saw. Later, I heard she lost her partner. Now she's troubled and nothing The Watch offered has helped. Devlin seems the logical solution."

"For both of them?"

Valentina met his look calmly. "He won't hurt her, Simon."

"Has it occurred to you your brother might refuse to take part in this cockamamie plan, Valentina?"

"You give the okay on Kate. I'll handle Devlin."

"You're that sure, are you?"

"Our brothers have never been capable of refusing Patience or me. Devlin's different now, but he won't say no."

The venerable commander of The Black Watch was equally as sure. Just as he'd known when she marched into his office with that familiar determined look that no matter what she wanted, or what argument he offered, he would lose.

"So," Valentina concluded. "If there's nothing else…"

"Haven't you overlooked something?"

Mission accomplished, she was ready to leave. "Have I?"

With a scrawl, he tore a sheet from a pad. "Kate's address."

"I know where she is, Simon."

Crumpling the paper, he muttered, "Given that her location is a deep secret, it seems I have a leak."

"There's no leak. My source talks only to me." A grin teased her mouth. "Unless you consider *me* the leak."

"Never you, Valentina." Drawing his thumb across a lighter, he touched flame to paper. When fire licked away letters spelling out Belle Terre, South Carolina, he dropped it in an empty trash can. "As usual, your visit has been…interesting."

"My pleasure."

"And mine."

Val paused by the door. "The standing invitation still stands, should you find time to come to the shore."

"I'll think about it."

"Positively, I hope." With a wave, she was gone.

Into the quiet, Simon spoke thoughtfully, "Maybe I will go out to the bay. Renew old acquaintances. Lay some groundwork."

The day was coming when he must choose his replacement. Given her intuition and with added maturity, Valentina O'Hara Courtenay would be the perfect choice. If she could succeed with Devlin in this, Simon hadn't a doubt she could do anything.

Ravenel's By The River was not just a grocery store, but also a meeting place for the citizenry of Belle Terre. Today, pleasant temperatures of autumn had brought shoppers out en masse. With music drifting about them, they traversed wide aisles, filling carts with an extraordinary array of wines, flowers, and groceries.

No one seemed to hurry. Some only nodded and smiled at other shoppers. But the majority stopped to chat, to gossip, to laugh, or to adjourn to the canopied balcony that served as a teahouse. There, with the river sliding by, in the shade of a centuries-old oak, they sipped tea, sherry, and even the ritual bourbon and branch water to the accompaniment of more gossip, more laughter.

Only Kate Gallagher seemed oblivious to the pleasant surroundings. Only she paid no homage to expected Southern customs as she moved through the music, gliding from one corridor to the next. Her head bent, her face veiled by a wealth of hair falling against her cheek, none who passed caught her eye. Some glanced her way. Others appeared inclined to speak. But as if the silvery veil were a wall innate courtesy must not breach, no one intruded.

Once upon a time Devlin O'Hara would have considered that aloof detachment a challenge. One look at the melancholy barely hidden in Kate's distracted gaze, and it would have become his prevailing mission in life to make her world a better place. To make her smile, perhaps even laugh, as the others laughed.

But that was once upon a time. A time of innocence now and forever lost to him. And no matter what he'd promise Valentina, he wouldn't interfere.

He'd learned that some things never heal, and the pain

and guilt never eased. Perhaps for some, as for him, it shouldn't.

If, as the cliché promised, the blind couldn't lead the halt, who was he to play Galahad?

And if the question had an answer, it wasn't one he wanted to face. Not now. Not yet. So it was that when she approached his loitering space, he turned away, determinedly immersing himself in deciding which brand of coffee he needn't buy.

He sensed her faltering step rather than heard it. Something more than the rustle of her clothing, or the scent of sunlight and flowers, warned of her nearness. An inexplicable awareness sent an uncommon disquiet racing through him.

More to counter any feelings regarding Valentina's latest lost lamb than an interest in the coffee he wouldn't be drinking on a Belle Terre morning, he reached for a brightly labeled packet. Unexpectedly, their hands collided, but his a fraction behind. With a pilot's instincts and reflexes, his fingers closed over hers, keeping the package from tumbling out of her grasp.

For a moment neither moved nor spoke. Devlin stared down at a mass of hair ranging from dark gold to the palest silver, and falling from a center part. Barely realizing he was holding his breath, he waited for her head to lift.

When she stirred, her unshielded gaze rising to his, her eyes were golden brown and fringed by dark lashes. Her look was remote, without emotion.

"Pardon me." Her voice was low and restrained, as remote, as emotionless, as her gaze. Each spare word was without accent, and perfectly enunciated in the quiet tone of a woman apart. A woman going through the motions of her life, taking each moment as it came. Coping...only coping.

Devlin was struck by the conviction that there should

be fire in those eyes. The light of the pleasure of life, the need of an accomplished woman to be all she had worked to be. Above all, there should be passion, desire, love, and contentment.

Wondering how glorious that gaze would be alight with love, he responded belatedly, "What is there to pardon?"

Turning from his study of her face to the packet they held jointly, Devlin's lips moved in a rare smile. "Unless preferring the same brand of coffee is a problem for you, Mrs....?"

The implied question seemed to fill the little space separating them. A simple question, but a look of haunting sadness altered the line of her lips. "It's Miss. I'm not married. As I suspect you've observed." Her voice was steady, hardly more than a breath. "And my name isn't important."

Devlin's smile, not the smile of old but one that would have set Valentina cheering, was undaunted. "Suppose I go first?"

"No." Her hair brushed over her shoulders with the slight shake of her head. "I don't mean to insult you, but who you are doesn't matter since it isn't likely we'll ever reach for the same package again. So, if you would give me back my hand, I'll take my bit of coffee and leave you to the rest of your shopping."

"I'm called Devlin."

"My hand, please." There was no anger in the reminder, no struggle to pull from his grasp.

"You're in a hurry?" His clasp didn't ease.

"My hand, please, Mr. Devlin."

"O'Hara." Devlin wasn't certain why he persisted, except that even anger would be an improvement over the lost, sad look.

"I beg your pardon?"

A spark of interest? Recognition of the name? Indignation? Or irritation, pure and simple? Whatever the reason, however coolly couched, he viewed a response of any sort as encouraging. "Devlin is my given name. O'Hara, my surname."

"Congratulations, Mr. O'Hara. I'm sure being a Devlin and an O'Hara is a marvelous experience." A bit of life, albeit small, flashed in her gaze. "Now, if you're through making a spectacle of both of us, I'd like to be on my way."

"Of course you would." Releasing her, with a small bow, he stepped back. "Have a good day, Lady Golden Eyes."

Making no acknowledgment of the name he'd bestowed in lieu of the name she'd refused him, she dropped the disputed package in a basket looped over her wrist. Without a hint of anger, she turned and walked away. He'd been dismissed, as if he'd never existed.

"Golden Eyes." He called softly, but not so softly she didn't hear. At her hesitant step, he said, "You forgot something."

Facing him, the frown line deepening between her brows, she let her gaze sweep over him, seeing more than a face and a hand for the first time. "I beg your pardon, Mr. O'Hara?"

The apology again. "You do that a lot, don't you?"

Her head tilted, her questioning look met his.

"Never mind." The grin that had been buried in grief for months warmed his face again. "It isn't important."

"In that case, I'll leave you to your shopping once more."

"The coffee." Devlin indicated the silver foil package in her basket. "I was here first, that package is mine."

"Yours...?" With a start, she looked down at her basket then back again at him. "Don't be ridiculous, there are others."

Devlin nodded. In recent neglect, his black hair had grown quite long—a lock fell over his forehead. Raking it back, he grinned again. "That's the one I picked, and that's the one I want."

This time no flicker of emotion showed in her face. "In that case." Taking the coffee from her basket, she returned to him. Taking his hand in hers, offering no comment on the scars marring his palm, she placed the packet in his grasp. "Be my guest, Mr. I'm-called-Devlin O'Hara."

Spinning about, she walked away, dismissing him again. He started to call out, to apologize, but he'd disturbed her enough for one day. Or any day, for he wouldn't be around for more.

He would keep to the letter of the half day he'd promised Valentina. Then he would turn his back on Belle Terre and the woman his sister thought could be saved.

"Perhaps she can." His lips barely moved, his words only a breath more than a thought. As he watched her move down the aisle, he remembered details he'd missed from afar—the frown line etched between her tawny brows, shadows lying like bruises beneath lightless eyes. The bittersweet tilt of a beautiful mouth.

A mouth meant for kisses, not sorrow.

While he struggled to put the errant thought aside, Devlin O'Hara felt a twinge of regret that he couldn't erase the frown, or put a sparkle back in her eyes. On impulse he'd called her Lady Golden Eyes, but he suspected that in moments of unbridled anger or love those eyes would be as bfiercely golden brown as a tigress's.

Against his will, his thoughts turned again to her lips. The gentle bow, the full under lip, as tawny pink as a rose petal moist with dew. How would her mouth look in a smile meant only for him? How would it feel beneath his? How sweet would she taste?

With more force than he intended, he dropped the coffee

in his basket. Even in his mind he wouldn't be lover or savior.

If she could be led back to the living, it wouldn't be by his hand. There was still fire banked there beneath the ice of grief and guilt. Hopefully someday she would be warmed enough by it to reach out and find her own way to resolution.

There was strength beneath the aloof veneer. Strength that allowed her to cut herself off from pain that might destroy her. So now she lived in limbo. For some, in the long run, it could be destructive...for others only a period of quiet healing.

Was that the key? Was Kate Gallagher a woman who sought a quiet life denied her? Perhaps that explained why her voice remained quiet and calm, whether she was or not. The outward control was a gift as well as a skill for one who had gone from mediating bitter arguments to leading a team of first response for The Black Watch.

How many countries, and how many volatile and unstable situations had she gone into? How many times had she risked her life, with only that skill and Paul Bryce to aid her? How many times had she been underestimated and misjudged? How many rebels and dissidents hadn't looked past the subdued decorum?

Valentina had called her Simon's best first weapon of choice. A dangerous trust, a treacherous and threatening existence. One that drew partners close, spurring unrivaled bonds. Even love.

Losing Paul Bryce would have been like losing a part of herself. Though she might heal in the self-imposed solitude, until she regained that part and rejoined the real world, Kate Gallagher would never be truly whole.

Like strength, spirit was there. He saw it in her face and her eyes. He heard it in her voice. Perhaps she was even halfway toward awakening it. Wanting only an intermediary, a person or a need, that would draw her the rest of the way.

Devlin could only hope that person, or that need, would come to her before it was too late. Before she settled into a life that was half what it should be.

As he watched her slipping unheeding past fellow shoppers, Devlin O'Hara held little hope the mentor she should have was among them. After months of living in Belle Terre, she was as much a stranger as he. Her wall of silence was too much for their native Southern gentility.

Suddenly he realized Kate had stepped to the checkout line, zipped through with her meager purchases, and was ready to leave. He'd followed and watched her discreetly for some time. After their encounter, if he continued much longer, despite her distraction she would become aware of his scrutiny. Even so, less because of his promise to Valentina than for reasons he couldn't explain, Devlin wasn't ready to step back and go away.

"No. Thank you, the flowers are lovely. But..." Her low voice shook him from his reverie. She'd paused by the door as she spoke to the tiny child who stood by an elderly lady and her pails and baskets filled with flowers of every sort imaginable. The bouquet the child offered was wrapped in a sheaf of green paper and surely contained at least one of each blossom.

The child said nothing as she held the bouquet out to Kate, a smile dimpling her cheeks.

"It would please her if you would take the flowers." The old woman's voice was quavery and weak. "God knows, there's little enough in her young life that's pleasing."

"But I haven't the proper change."

"The flowers are a gift," the woman interrupted. "Tessa hopes they might keep you from looking so sad."

Kate hesitated.

"Please," the woman pleaded.

From the place he'd taken in the express line, Devlin could see the sudden glitter of tears in Kate's eyes. Looking from the young, handsome woman to the fair child who could have been her daughter, he found himself praying she would accept the flowers, for all their sakes.

Though few of his prayers had been answered of late, his heart lifted when Kate knelt before the silent child. Taking the flowers, solemnly she kissed a dimpled cheek. "Thank you, Tessa. I've never had a bouquet or a present as lovely."

Tessa ducked her head shyly, saying nothing. Even when Kate said goodbye, the child didn't look up or speak.

"Have a good day, ma'am." The lady spoke for both.

"Thank you." Kate paused at the exit. Stroking the flowers across her cheek, she smiled. A blinding, wonderful smile. "How could I not?"

Devlin caught his breath, dazzled by the woman he'd glimpsed. The woman Kate Gallagher must be again. Impulsively, he moved toward her. An insistent voice called him back.

"Your change, sir. And your coffee."

"Keep it." Eager for another glimpse of that woman, he flung the words over his shoulder.

"I can't, sir. Please." The clerk's plea was plaintive, even disturbed. "It would mean my job."

Impatient, Devlin returned to the counter. He wanted neither change nor coffee. The purchase had been justification for time spent in the store, an excuse to stay close to Kate. Taking up the coins, mindful not to forget his purchase lest he be summoned back again, he hurried to the exit. Pausing to tweak a golden curl and wink down at little Tessa, he stepped into the street in time to see the lady of his concern drive away.

He'd come to the coastal town because he'd given his

word. All he intended was a quick trip from the Chesapeake, a short stay and a quicker look at Valentina's latest lamb. Then, home.

If there was such a place.

Quickly in, quickly away. An ironclad plan, with no expectations of more. But that was before he'd seen Kate Gallagher.

"'The best-laid schemes o'mice and men gang aft a-gley,'" he quoted in a muttered undertone. All for a smile.

Could he leave now? With a ghost of the rueful grin that had once set every young heart it touched aflutter, he mocked his own frailty. "I must. I should. But how, Lady Golden Eyes?"

Two

Music washed over him, ebbing and flowing like the tide lapping at his feet. In the time he'd sat on the derelict palmetto washed from another shore, the mood of the pianist changed. From tentative beginnings the tempo had gradually quickened, then swelled, filling this secluded section of shore with its moods.

First it was wild with the violence of unspeakable torment. Next, fiercely angry, each note resounding as if the musician fought the music, the instrument, and herself. Then the temperament changed, quieted. In slow, muted notes despair reached a deeper level, and Devlin heard the throb of anguish that defied solace.

As the piano fell silent, one note lingering in the night, he knew he'd been given rare insight into the heart of Kathleen Moira Gallagher, daughter of a roving diplomat. Once a model and an icon of beauty, a gifted pianist and a lawyer, an agent of The Black Watch and Simon's mediator par excellence, now she was simply a grieving woman whose soul stumbled.

When he'd followed her surreptitiously from Ravenel's to Summer Island, the gated, guarded seasonal playground of the wealthy of Belle Terre, it was to quiet a need he thought had died forever on Denali. To subdue a faltering, resurrected impulse to ease the hurts of others, he'd come to make himself believe he, least of all, could lead her back into the life she should have.

A simple matter, quickly done. So he hoped. Instead he'd tarried long in this single day he'd promised Valentina he would devote to Kate Gallagher. Tramping from one end of the somnolent paradise to the other, seeking proof of peace, the healing panacea Kate needed, he'd delayed and detoured, exploring marshes, docks, and the house that would have been his. Had he decided to stay.

Before he was ready, before innate urges were stifled, night had fallen. With the lights of Belle Terre sparkling in the near distance, the moon lifted over sea and shore like a great gold and silver globe. Silver and gold, the color of her hair. A reminder he didn't want. And, without intending it, he'd found himself on this part of the shore, sitting at the base of zigzagging steps leading where he'd never meant to go. To Kate.

When the first note sounded, he'd turned from it. The step away wouldn't come. He willed himself not to stay. He had.

Crouching on the salt-scoured palmetto, he listened.

Now the shore was quiet, the spell of her music ended. He was free to go. He knew he wouldn't. "The blind and the halt, Kate." He stared up at her house and the light that left more in darkness than it illuminated. "We shall see where one leads the other."

He turned again, truly leaving this time, but only to make the calls that would confirm his stay on Summer

Island. As he moved deeper into darkness, away from the little light, he didn't notice the woman on the deck above. He didn't see her drifting like a waif down the steps to the shore. He didn't know she knelt in the sand contemplating his footprints as if they would tell a story. Or that when she stood, it was to search him out with a puzzled frown, studying the familiar lines of his retreating figure.

"No." Out of habit Kate pressed the heels of her hands against her temples. The insidious thrum of tension was there. The encounter with the dangerously attractive but enormously annoying man hadn't helped. Then, as if that weren't enough, Jericho Rivers, sheriff of Belle Terre and the surrounding county, called to say the island might soon have another resident.

In the confusion of the abrupt interruption by an emergency call, Jericho hadn't given her a name, but managed to assure her that the newcomer was a friend, a good man. High praise from the taciturn sheriff. Surely it stretched the realm of coincidence to imagine the man in the grocer's and Jericho's friend were the same.

It couldn't be. Letting her hair fly in the wind, Kate remembered Devlin O'Hara. The mischievous look, his fascinating eyes at odds with his smile. A deep voice with an edge of uncertainty, as if it had been a while since he'd laughed or teased.

Despite her annoyance, she hadn't been blind to his charm. Or was it that he was charming and she noticed that annoyed her? Did it matter? The new islander wouldn't be Devlin O'Hara.

If it should be, they needn't meet again. Though the land mass was considered small with three miles of beach, there were only six houses lining the shore. The property of each was bounded on the west by the narrow river separating the marsh from the mainland, and on the east by the sea. With each possessing docks on the riverside and decks at the front with promenades to the shore. Trailing north to south, each house was set in the middle of a half-mile tract. Except Sea Watch, her home in recent months.

Indulging a penchant for privacy, the owner of Sea Watch set his house on the southernmost tip, where sea and river merged. Thus, with nearly a mile setting the house apart from the others, she needn't trip over anyone.

"No matter who he is." Peering after him, she discovered he'd moved beyond the natural curve of the island and out of sight. That was as she wanted him.

Keeping solitary spaces had never been difficult. Falling within the domain of Belle Terre, the island was populated exclusively by local residents. Townies, wealthy enough to keep second homes for the island's namesake season. Most houses were closed for the year and for the social season the first of August.

Some of the owners returned for rare weekends. Others for Thanksgiving and Christmas. Except for that possible influx, with Hobie, the elderly guard, controlling the mainland gate and protecting against interlopers, Kate had what she counted the best of all seasons virtually to herself. Until now.

There was no need to waste time in worry. Two did not constitute a crowd. The bastion of water and sand that kept the world away needn't change.

"He won't." As a gust of wind swept the words from her lips, Kate clenched a fist. "One man won't change my life."

A lonely figure caught in moonlight, she crossed the sand. It was late, she was tired. But as she climbed the steps, she knew she was not tired enough. Tonight she'd played long and forcefully, and still the music failed her. Neither its therapy nor exhaustion numbed her mind.

Retracing her steps, she entered the house, intent on closing it for the night. For a half hour she moved about restlessly, avoiding the inevitable. When there was no more to be done, she drifted to a window to watch the surf, to lose herself in the alternately dark and luminous rhythm. Hopefully, to forget.

Longer than was prudent, she watched the wash of waves. Sometimes the past intruded, with thoughts of Paul Bryce. Other times she thought of nothing. Once, she recalled the solitary figure whose footprints told a story of pausing beneath her window. Had he stayed to listen, or only to rest before walking on?

The newcomer, roaming farther afield than she wished. A stranger on the beach that had been hers alone.

A good man, the sheriff had assured her. Jericho wouldn't lie. And the stranger did not trespass. The beach belonged to everyone. As she conceded that reality, Kate realized the hour had gone from late to early. It was time to face her demons.

Turning out the lamp, she went to her bed knowing sleep would not come quickly. When it came, because the music failed, it would not be blessedly dreamless.

Sun streamed through an open window striking unshielded eyes with a vengeance. Throwing an arm over her face, Kate pondered her day. But what was there to ponder? What would be different? She would rise, sit on the deck drinking endless cups of coffee, hoping to stave off the threat of a migraine. While she drank, she would watch shorebirds strafe for their first meal of the day. After her own meager breakfast, more homage to a habit than for nutrition, she would tramp the land for hours.

She might collect shells, she might not. Maybe she would gather driftwood, maybe not. But she would climb the tallest dune. There, she would watch herons and egrets moving in the grasses of the marsh and through the surf. Perhaps she would catch a glimpse of a night heron, home late from a long hunt. Or the elusive green, that favored the minnows in the tidal pool beneath the dune.

Then there were the dolphins, sleek, graceful, common in the autumn season. ''And the whales.''

Enthusiasm colored her voice as she braved the sun. Would they be back? Days before, on her morning ramble, she had sighted them. Two mammoths of the sea, cavorting in the still warm waters of the Carolina coast. Yesterday, after her trip into town, she hadn't looked for them again. But maybe today.

Rolling out of bed more eagerly than she had in longer than she could remember, she threw on a shirt and dashed to the kitchen. A rattle of canisters and cabinet doors later, she stopped short. No coffee. Which meant no caffeine. Leaning against the cabinet, she recalled the day before.

''I gave it to him.'' Then, hurrying from Ravenel's and the crowd, she'd forgotten all about coffee.

No problem. Lifting a shoulder, she shrugged aside the error. There were other remedies or other ways. Even a return trip to Ravenel's, this time with no Devlin O'Hara to set her in flight.

But that day hadn't been a total loss. She had met Tessa. A glance at the bouquet standing in a teal and copper vase on the kitchen counter drew an uncommon smile from Kate.

The child was exquisite with her blond curls atumble, brown eyes shining. Could even Scrooge have refused her flowers? Touching them, Kate remembered the old lady's words…. *A gift. Tessa hopes the flowers might keep you from looking so sad.*

As she remembered, Kate realized she was smiling. Yesterday, Tessa had made her smile. And now again, she was truly smiling. In that moment, the darkness in her heart weighed a little less heavily, her thoughts were clearer.

Tea! Tea would be a nice change. "How long has it been?"

A knock at the door interrupted her monologue—a habit she'd fallen into during the days she spent alone. Strange. But not so strange as morning visitors, she decided as she went to answer.

Her smile vanished as she opened the door. "You!"

Before she could stop them, suspicions she'd spent an evening denying spilled out. "It was you on the beach last night."

"Devlin O'Hara, ma'am, paying a neighborly call." As he inclined his head slightly, his hair falling over his forehead gleamed blacker than black.

"Neighborly." Kate crossed her arms before her, remembering the state of her nightclothes. "Which, I suppose by association of words, means we're to be neighbors."

"For now," he amended. "Only for a while."

His smile was the same, but with the light of morning falling on his face, she realized any expression left his remarkable eyes untouched. Was there a coldness beneath the banter, or an unfeeling void?

Whichever, it wasn't her concern, and the sooner he went away, the better. "Ahh, so for only a while we're to be neighbors. I suppose that means you've come to borrow a cup of sugar?"

"Not this time. I'll save that for later." If he felt the cut of her mockery, it didn't show. His smile altered, his mouth curving generously. Taking his hand from behind his back, he produced the foil packet of coffee. "I have two, so I came to share."

"You're so sure I need a share?" There might be no emotion in his eyes, but his piercing gaze missed little. Barely resisting the urge to smooth her hair into order, she caught at her shirt, drawing it closer about her breasts.

Leaning an arm on the doorjamb, his forehead resting on his wrist, he looked down at her. "You left Ravenel's without any."

Kate wasn't short, but in her bare feet, the upward tilt of her head required to meet his gaze was significant. As he shifted positions, the sun striking her face turned him into a looming shadow. A ploy to hide his expression, or lack of it? Was Devlin O'Hara far more complicated than he seemed? A man guarding secrets? But if there were secrets, they were none of her concern.

"Ahh, I see," she drawled, matching his projected mood. "I left the store empty-handed, so to speak. Which led you to assume my coffee coffer is bare?"

He didn't take his gaze from her. "Would you have been in Belle Terre otherwise?"

"Touché, Mr. O'Hara. You're very astute."

"I have my days."

"Yes, you do, don't you? This time you were right." As she took the package, her fingers brushing his, she said in genuine sincerity, "Thank you."

In answer, he touched his brow in a small salute. "Enjoy, Miss Gallagher. And have a good day."

Kate watched his retreat. For all his rugged handsomeness and wicked teasing, she sensed a devastating sorrow hidden deeply within him. An unshakable conviction she couldn't explain. Intuition? Compassion? The wisdom of one wounded soul recognizing another, when once she would have been blinded to it? The incredible certainty that no matter that they were strangers, they were no different? In the end, was it knowing in some strange way that, as she, he had not yet found the peace that must come with healing?

Surprised by that bit of wisdom, touched by his kindness in the throes of trouble, Kate called out, "A question, Mr. O'Hara."

He stopped at the end of the deck, his hand on the railing, one foot on the first step. A stance that rippled the shirt clinging to his shoulders, emphasizing the flat plane of his midriff. His arms and face were tanned, the brand of a life spent out of doors.

In wind and water? Sun or snow? If she were to guess his age, she would say thirty-six. Maybe thirty-eight. Would that mean he was a veteran sailor? Aging surfer? Jaded ski bum? As her mind formed the thoughts, she was discarding them. No doubt any of the three would be too tame for him, even though he waited patiently, as if he had all the time in the world for her. "You don't really have any extras, do you?"

"Extras?" He lifted an innocent brow. Too innocent.

"Coffee, Mr. O'Hara." Kate waggled the package. "You don't have even one extra, do you?"

He took a deep breath, his chest lifting and straining harder against the seams of his shirt. "No, ma'am, I don't."

Once Kate would have thought the repetitious title was sly mockery. But given the way he used it, the easy flow of it in his speech, she was almost certain it was an intended courtesy. *Ma'am,* the contraction of *madam,* a title of honor for a lady. Something learned long ago, no doubt, and deeply ingrained.

"I make a good cup. Will you join me, Mr. O'Hara?"

"Thanks." He hesitated. "But I've intruded enough."

Minutes ago, Kate would have agreed. Now, in an about-face, she didn't want him to go. "You haven't intruded. In fact, I'd like some company. For one morning, at least."

Devlin smiled then, the same half smile. The lady was smooth. In one breath she'd been gracious and hospitable, and in the next closed the door firmly against repeat performances.

His decision to stay on the island was unexpected, and he was without a clue how to begin with her. He'd come today out of conscience, but hoping to find a chink in her armor. The invitation had taken him unaware. Yet it was a beginning, and he'd learned a man never won points with a lady by refusing an invitation. "Then it would be my pleasure for one morning. But there is a condition."

"What would that be, Mr. O'Hara?"

"That you call me Devlin."

"Only if you call me Kate."

"Done." He laughed then. A warm, wonderful sound.

"In that case, Devlin O'Hara, will you join me for coffee?"

Not quite as he asked, but close. "Yes, ma'am, I will."

"Then it's settled." Stepping away from the door, Kate led him to the great room. "Make yourself comfortable. I'll start the coffee—while it's brewing I'll catch a shower and change."

"A pity."

He hadn't gone into the sitting area, but had followed her closely. So closely that when she faced him, she was exquisitely aware that he smelled pleasantly of soap and sea mists. A thoroughly masculine scent that fit him perfectly. Trying not to stare or breathe, she backed away and found herself hemmed in by cabinets and his lean, virile body. Blinking, she looked up at him. "A pity?"

"You look fetching in your nightclothes." Catching the neck of her T-shirt between thumb and forefinger, he let the banded fabric roll beneath his touch. "A Clemson University Tiger T-shirt and an orange overshirt." Moving his hand to the overshirt, he drew the collar closer about her throat. "Silk, unless I miss my guess. A combination I don't think I've seen before."

Laying the package aside, Kate leaned back, bracing against the counter, creating an inch more space between them. "Should I take that to mean you're accustomed to spending your mornings with ladies in nightclothes? Elegant, garish, or otherwise."

"No," Devlin replied solemnly. "You should assume I have sisters, who would envy you this."

Kate laughed, suddenly at ease, as he intended. "What you mean is, they would envy my nerve, or faint dead away at the sight."

"Maybe." Devlin wondered if she had any idea what the vivid colors did for her eyes. In his mind she was a tigress. Once she *had* been, in looks and spirit. She would be again. "Tell you what, I'll make the coffee, you go do whatever..."

"That sounds like a plan." Relieved without knowing why, she slipped past him. Yet, in her dash for the security of the bath, she paused. "You can find what you need?"

"I'll muddle my way through."

"I imagine you're good at that. Muddling, I mean. Making the best of a situation."

"I have been. I was." A shadow crossed his face. "Once."

Troubled by the quick change, Kate waited for more. When there was none, she hurried away.

"Sorry I took so long," Kate said as she stepped onto the deck. What she saw there was astonishing. In less than twenty minutes, Devlin had not merely made coffee. He'd plundered the refrigerator, the pantry and the property owner's linen closet.

In the time she'd been in residence, she'd spared the closets only a cursory glance. She knew there were fine linens of all colors and an assortment of table settings to boggle the mind, but she was reluctant to use them. Obviously, her astonishing and accomplished guest felt no such reluctance.

"Hello." Looking up from the table he'd set, he let his gaze sweep over her. If orange became her, a turquoise shirt tucked into white slacks was spectacular. If it weren't for remnants of fatigue marking her features, she could return to the runway of any fashion house in the world.

"You were going to make coffee." Kate moved to his side.

"I did."

"But this." A gesture encompassed the table, crystal and silver glittering in the sun. Napkins—of linen, no less. A salad of fruit she'd stashed in the fridge and forgotten. With what appeared to be a pitcher of mimosas. Best of all, Tessa's flowers sat in the center of the table. "This looks like a celebration."

"Maybe." Drawing out a chair, he waited, silently, until she had no choice but to take the offered seat.

Wondering what the most attractive man she'd ever seen, but with the saddest eyes, would find to celebrate, Kate's gaze followed as he returned to stand across from her. Sipping from a glass he'd filled for her, discovering it was truly a mimosa, she watched him over the glittering rim before setting the glass aside.

Forgetting that as recently as yesterday she wouldn't have noticed any man, attractive or not, she settled back. And with a long, slow look, Kate Gallagher committed to memory all that made Devlin O'Hara an intriguing man.

Ranging over the little not masked by table and flowers, her gaze touched first on his hair. Darker than she believed possible, longer than she liked as a rule. But on Devlin, the shaggy look of disregard was seductive, especially when it capped craggy features that spoke of a life of adventure. Eyes like blue topaz with barely masked anguish lurking in their depths, and a mouth that could be grim and beautiful at once, completed an aura of compelling magnetism and extraordinary sensuality.

Compelling, extraordinary, and unstudied. It hadn't taken long to understand that nothing about Devlin was calculated. How he looked, how he talked, the frisson of sexual tension he exuded, were natural. Part and parcel of a man who would be irresistible…if she'd met him in another time, another place. If both hadn't brought the inescapable baggage of terminal grief along with them.

Watching as he spooned a colorful array of fruits into brandy snifters, then topped each with a bit of cream, she wondered when and where he'd learned to be so creative in the kitchen.

Had he been married? Was he still?

Of course not. Kate was certain there was no woman in Devlin O'Hara's life. But had there been? Had he lost someone beloved? Did that explain the grief she saw in him? And, perchance, his palms?

He made no effort to hide the scars, but something in his demeanor warned discussion was off limits. As someone with her own secret hurts, Kate would never pry. When, or if, he wanted her to know, he would tell her. She would not question, until then.

Or never. He'd said he would stay for a while. For all she knew, "for a while" meant only this day.

"Something wrong?" he asked. "You don't like mimosas?

"I beg your pardon?" Kate was so engrossed in her thoughts, she only half heard him.

"You were frowning. I asked if there's something wrong."

Kate sat a little straighter, improvising. "Only that I'm sitting like a dolt, when I should help."

"No help needed." His piercing gaze traced the lines of her face. "You're too lovely to be a dolt. So, sit in the sun. Rest while I finish, then we'll share our first meal."

"I am rested." With the flush of his compliment on her

cheeks, she knew it was true. "More rested than in a long time."

"No dreams last night? Or only good ones?"

The question surprised her, making her wonder how he could know she dreamed, and in those dreams faced her demons night after night. But as quickly, she knew he asked because it was the same for him. Devlin had his own battle in the dark. But the lasting surprise was her recollection that it was Devlin who strolled through her dreams, smiling his half smile and teasing, then disappearing into a glittering moonlit sea.

"I dreamed," she admitted. "But only good ones."

Circling the table he set her salad in place. As he leaned near her, his fingers curled briefly over hers. "Any night without the troubles that stalk us is a good night, isn't it, Kate?"

Looking at him, golden gaze meeting blue, with his clean scent a part of every breath, the beat of her heart thundered in her veins. He was so close, she saw the creases radiating from his eyes. Laugh lines. The mark of a man who once had enjoyed life. A man who understood her, for the life he lived now was the same.

Though he was a stranger who had appeared on her doorstep, she wanted to reach out to him, to comfort him. But she hadn't the right. "A night without troubles is a gift I don't deserve."

"I doubt that," Devlin countered gently, then said no more, for it wasn't time. They were moving too fast. One wrong step and doors that opened a sliver would close to him forever. "Enough serious stuff. Agreed, Lady Golden Eyes?"

The silly name drew a reluctant smile. "Agreed."

"Then, one last touch and breakfast is served." Drawing a flower from Tessa's bouquet, he snapped the stem and tucked the creamy blossom in her hair. "A pretty flower for a pretty lady."

His hand lingered at her cheek in a caressing touch. So much in his life was harsh and unforgiving, he only wanted to feel a bit of softness. Just a bit.

"Kate."

"Devlin?"

She'd never said his name like that. Never called him simply Devlin. He wanted to hear it again and again in that low, calm voice while the sun and the sea spun their magic around her.

"When I came, I didn't intend to stay. I promised myself one night..." He faltered over the half-truth. Devlin who never lied, who never feared anything, was afraid he would hurt her. Afraid his presence would ruin the island for her and destroy the little contentment she'd found.

"The island is a pretty, peaceful place. I've seen a lot of the world, yet I didn't expect what I found here. Even so, I won't intrude, I won't stay, Kate. If you don't want me here."

She waited through his little speech, hearing words of praise she'd said when she first came. She heard him voice the fears she'd felt when Jericho warned of a stranger in her paradise.

She knew Devlin would go, if she asked. Yesterday, it would have been what she wanted. Now she heard herself saying, "Summer Island is big enough for two. Our paths needn't cross."

Devlin pretended nonchalance. "I suppose not."

"But today they have, thanks to neighborly kindness."

"This was presumptuous. Rummaging through your supplies and food. Dragging out table linens. Robbing a superb wine cellar."

"Letting good food go to waste," Kate added to his list. "With generously shared coffee growing cold. Sit down,

Devlin. What you've done is not an intrusion. Yes, I've had the island to myself, but it isn't mine, you know.''

"Two isn't a crowd?''

"Let's take it one day at a time, and see how it goes.''

"Then I'll stay, Kate. One day at a time.''

Devlin sat across from her. Listening as she told him of the island creatures and their habits, he discovered she hadn't spent her reclusive life moldering. She was observant, well read. Well versed, even expert, in the history of the area.

"Once Summer Island was called after Stede Bonnet?'' he prompted, to hear her speak, to listen to softly elegant tones.

"This was Bonnet's hunting ground. Anchoring on the backside of the island, the gentleman pirate waited for his prey. Hopefully, he was a better gentleman than a pirate. After he was hanged in Charleston, the name was forgotten. Now some call it Summer Island. To others, though there are dozens of islands scattered along this coastline, it's simply *the* island.'' Grimacing, she said, "That's enough instruction for one day.''

"You make it interesting.''

"And you're a gentleman and a liar.''

"Thank you, ma'am. I treasure the compliment.''

They drifted into a companionable silence, broken only by the clatter of palmettos catching a breeze. Kate was first to speak. "There were whales off the point day before yesterday. They don't come often. When they do, they stay for some time. I'll show you the best dune for observing, if you like.''

She offered it like a gift. Rising to go to her, drawing her from her own chair and keeping her hand in his, Devlin murmured, "I'd like that. I'd like it very much.''

The reclusive Kate had reached out. But he wasn't fooled. With the sea at their feet and an autumn sun to warm them, a man and a woman who were more than strangers, but not yet friends, might spend a pleasant morning walking the beach. But there would be dark times ahead for both of them. Times when Denali came for him in his dreams. Times when Kate fought her demons and herself with night music.

But someday, for Kate, there would be times of peace.

Three

A sharp report splintered the air, followed by a rapid barrage impacting like gunshots against Kate's ears. Recoiling instinctively, she tumbled from her seat, a paperback novel flying from her lap. Crouching on the weathered dock, she braced for more.

But there was no more. Quiet settled over a peaceful day as if it had never been broken. A flock of ibis, erupted from the limbs of a bald cypress by the first battering sound, began to return. Croaking raucously in a show of indignation, each perched precariously again in a great flap of wings and flying feathers. Once settled, wings tucked, feathers soothed, only their low grousing and the lazy lap of the river marked the passage of the day.

Birds ceased their muttering, the river sped to the sea undisturbed. As the midmorning sun burned hotly over the dock of Sea Watch, the well of quiet deepened, only to be broken by a humorless, restless laugh.

Rising, dusting sand and splinters away, Kate shrugged in disgust. After joining The Black Watch, she'd endured months of training. Grueling, precise drills teaching and preparing her to deal with any situation. The skills Simon McKinzie required were drummed into her. Drummed and tested, until each merged with natural abilities. Becoming first nature, as Simon promised, not second.

And still she sprawled on the dock at the clap of a hammer.

Thankfully, only the birds witnessed the clumsy and comical display. "Okay, guys, you don't tell, I won't."

Abashed by the added foolishness of bargaining with ibis, Kate collected her book and settled again into her effort to read. But the pages were only a collection of words. Words of little sense, requiring no flock of startled ibis to be lost to her.

When the hammer sounded again, she was ready for it. She knew then why the book was just words, and the words never a story.

Devlin. Lately of Summer Island.

He'd kept his promise. A week had passed since their paths crossed. If he'd returned to the point seeking the whales again, it was never when she'd gone. If he walked the beach, he kept from sight. If he listened when she played through the night and into morning, it was from a distant point, beyond the muted light.

The island was as it had always been. She was alone. Yet how many times had she looked up, hoping he would be there? How many times had she turned, thinking to share some seashore treasure?

How many times in her dreams had Paul Bryce segued into Devlin O'Hara. Why had they become tangled in her mind?

Devlin. He'd come first as an interloper, a teasing stranger. Next, as the thoughtful neighbor. A day on the

beach made him a friend. Like the best kind of friend, he'd
honored his word.

The hammer pounded. Kate remembered a sagging dock
damaged by tides and time, and knew he was repairing it.

Devlin made promises and kept them. She had made
none, and had none to keep. Tossing the book aside and
catching up the sundress she often wore over bathing suits,
Kate went in search of shoes. Then a little sunscreen on
her nose, moisturizer for her lips, a band to hold back her
hair, and she was ready for her first neighborly visit.

A thought and a detour to the kitchen delayed her journey. But days on the island were timeless, marked only by
the rise of the sun and the setting of the moon. What did
she have but time? Too much time to brood. From the
look in his somber eyes, what did he?

The walk was a bit over a mile, if one counted the small
jogs from the water's edge to the dunes to investigate suspected treasures. The basket she carried grew heavy, but
she didn't mind. What better way to ease tired arms and
a restive mind than browsing tidal pools, while the basket
languished on the sand?

The deep thud of the hammer served as her beacon. The
sound was rhythmic, with evenly timed breaks. Enough to
fetch a board, or smooth a rough edge. Long enough, she
supposed, for a hungry man to wolf down a sandwich or
soft drink. Considering that the sun was approaching its
zenith, a definite possibility.

Amazingly, Kate didn't care. For too long she'd worried
about every little detail of every little thing. The worry
weighing her down like a burden. But today, with different
worries lying like a wound on her heart, the small hap-
penstances didn't matter. If he'd eaten by the time she
arrived, the meal could be put in the fridge. After a long
day of laboring in the sun, a shrimp salad sandwich and a

glass of white wine should go down smooth and easy with twilight.

The staccato beat of the hammer set the tempo as she climbed the steps leading to Devlin. The rambling structure of the oldest house on the island stood on pilings hidden by lattice. Through checkered openings she could see him, naked to the waist, a bandanna tied about his forehead, sweat gleaming on straining muscles.

He moved like a dancer, but without flourish or conspicuous display. He was simply a man doing a job, and doing it well.

In the shadows beneath the house, Kate stopped to watch, recognizing as never before that a man at work was a thing of beauty.

Amused by the poetic vision, she grasped the basket tighter, stepped past the house, skirted the pool, and crossed the back lawn to the dock. With each step she discovered that he was more than beautiful. Yet with a rough edge to his magnetism, an intensity bespeaking strength and virility. An intriguing brawny power in the leanness of his body and the startling width of his shoulders.

His jeans were aged and tattered, the faded color more white than blue. The denim, worn thin, embraced like fragile silk. When he planted his booted feet, hefting an oversize support in place then walking it upright, there was little doubt the brawn and virility applied to every inch of Devlin O'Hara.

Kate had never been a jock watcher. In college she hadn't understood the groupie mentality of classmates who drooled over athletes, or swooned at a smile from the fraternity chaps. Devlin wasn't a college athlete, she suspected he had been too much the maverick for fraternities, but at the ripe old age of thirty-three, she was beginning to understand those long-ago classmates.

A terminal case of delayed adolescence? Groaning, Kate shifted the basket and wondered if she'd lost her mind. Paul Bryce had been as handsome, as virile, yet he'd never intrigued her.

"Hello, Kate."

"Devlin, good morning." Kate was pleased with the casual greeting, except that it was afternoon now.

If he noticed the mispoken time he didn't comment. His welcoming gesture was natural, as if she appeared on his doorstep every day with a basket clutched in her hands. A morning in the sun had laid another layer of tan on his face, and the flash of his smile was lightning reaching out to strike.

The new darkness of his features made his eyes bluer. If the stunning smile ever touched them, he would be devastating.

"Sorry for the ruckus." Droplets of sweat gleaming, veins standing like ropes beneath bronzed skin, he made the apology sincerely. "This is something I felt I needed to do."

As a favor to Hank McGregor, the owner? Kate wondered. Or because he needed to work? "Rain and a rough tide undermined the pilings again several weeks ago. I intended to call Mr. McGregor, but when Jericho was out on patrol, he said he would."

"He did." One last push, and the brace was in place. Patting the rough wood, and swiping the sweat from his forehead with his arm, Devlin faced her. "I figure the least I can do in return for use of the house, is to make the repairs."

"You know Mr. McGregor?"

Sliding the bandanna from his head, Devlin mopped his throat and chest with it. "Only through Jericho"—with a quirk of his lips, as he picked up a hammer—"I knew he was a character when I realized what he'd named the house.''

''You've deciphered the sign out front?''

''I think so.'' Finished with putting his tools away, Devlin took the basket from her, hefting it in his hand. ''Lunch?''

''If you like.''

Taking her arm, his fingers closing over the soft, bare flesh, he led her to a puddle of shade beneath a palmetto. ''Give me a minute to clean up, darlin', and I'll show you how much I like.''

The memory of his touch tingling against her arm, Kate watched as he strolled to the house. Watched as the sun struck an iridescent sheen on his skin, and worn jeans clung as faithfully to his rear as his thighs. No bravado, no theater, the honest sweat and the favored clothing of a man at work, with no thought to entice.

Kate had no doubt he could be a master at the art of beguiling, but she found his uncontrived appeal far more disarming. She'd grown surprisingly comfortable with Devlin in a short time. A rare circumstance, one that would never have happened if he'd made a great show of his charm and gallantry.

Or was that part of his mystique? Did he tailor his manner to the woman? That there had been women was a forgone conclusion. How many were lovers? How many friends? Would he understand that a friend was what she needed? All she wanted?

''Deep thoughts?'' He stood at her side, his hair damp and brushed back. In that little time, he'd slipped on a shirt, stuffed a fresh bandanna in a pocket, and changed into jeans a little less faded, a little less enamored of his masculinity.

Looking up, she met the unsmiling gaze. ''Not so deep.''

His mouth moved in concern. "Important thoughts, then."

"Sorry. Nothing deep. Nothing important." Kate's denial was reiterated by the barest shake of her head. A denial, and a lie that made no sense. Caught in a quagmire of grief and guilt, she'd lived the life of a recluse for months, resisting every offer of comfort and every friendly overture. Then Devlin came. Generous, wicked, teasing Devlin with his ready smile, and his sad eyes. And in him she saw a kindred soul, and a friend.

Dragging out a chair, he sat across from her, his hands folded on the table. Instead of pursuing her comment, he changed subjects smoothly. "I was hoping you would come by."

"You were? Why?"

"Because I wanted to see you." His fingers flexed and tightened over each other. "I wanted it to be your choice."

"I'm here, Devlin." Her tone was rueful. "I don't understand why. But understanding, or not, the choice was mine."

"Don't try to understand, Kate. Just play this slow and easy, letting each day bring what it will." Linking a finger through hers, he grinned. "I hope today brought good company and a feast for a famished man."

"I suppose that makes this the first day we take as it comes…to see what it brings." Kate didn't react to his touch, nor did she take her hand away. "Shall we begin with the basket?"

"Darlin'." He clasped her hand briefly in his. "I thought you'd never ask."

Kate set out the simple meal, then sat back to watch. If she feared bringing the meal was a mistake, he set her mind at ease by the sheer pleasure with which he ate.

His appetite was good, but from the slenderness that left corded muscles almost too exquisitely defined, she doubted that was always the case. "More?" She offered her own sandwich as he finished his second. "Or there's cheesecake from the freezer."

"Can't." Leaning back, he flexed a shoulder and sighed. "I'd like to sit here awhile, just listening to you."

"Listening to me?" Kate was startled by the comment. "Why on earth would you want that?"

"Because I like your voice. Clear and soothing, calm, even when you're not." He saw her tense, but gave no indication he had. "I swear, I believe you're proof of the legend."

His charisma might be uncalculated, but he wasn't above pure blarney. "What legend would that be, Mr. O'Hara?"

"Charming birds out of trees, darlin'. With that low, sweet voice." The teasing was gone from his tone, the contentment from his look. "Talk to me, Kate. Charm me, just for a little while."

Make me forget.

He didn't say the words, but she heard them as surely as if he had. He was tired, likely dehydrated, and a half bottle of wine hadn't helped. She wanted to refuse, but couldn't. Just as she couldn't bristle at the casual endearment, as she would have once upon another time. Thinking to inject the safety of formality into the familiar, she began, "What would you like me to say, Mr....?"

"Don't, Kate," he interrupted quietly. "Don't call me Mister. We've a long way to go, but we've come past that."

"All right." Clasping her hands in her lap, she began again. "What would you like me to say, Devlin?"

"Anything."

"Anything," she mused, casting about for a subject. Recalling a lone sign on the dune by the steps, she found the topic of what she intended to be a short monologue. "Turtles."

Beneath the piercing gaze that never left her lips, she continued, "There's a loggerhead nest beyond the Sea Watch. A late hatching nest. Which is one of the reasons I keep the lights low."

Catching his gaze, she asked, "You do know the hatchlings follow bright lights, and could wander away from the sea?"

Devlin ducked his head, once, acknowledging that he knew, but reluctant to break the flow of her voice.

"The rest hatched, except one other by Scotch and Water."

Drawn from rapt attention, he mused, "Scotch and Water?"

"This house." Her gesture implied the space around them. "Your house. Every place on the island has a sign with its name. McGregor was more inventive, and twice as secretive. Hobie, the guard, says it's fun to watch folks figure out the two signs. One McGregor plaid."

"One solid blue," he finished for her.

"Most who know McGregor by reputation or name only, assume it stands for a Scot by the sea. Those who know him more intimately, choose Scotch and Water."

"McGregor's drink of choice," Devlin supplied, and the half smile was back. The man was plainly a character, exactly the sort who would think nothing of turning his summer home over to the friend of a friend. No questions asked. But that was the sort of friend who was drawn to Simon McKinzie. The sort of friend he trusted and treasured. Devlin's smile became a chuckle. "So he sits back, sips his Scotch and water, and watches the fun."

"That's the way Hobie tells it."

"I like how Hobie tells it."

"So do I." Her story done, Kate fell silent.

"Don't stop."

Laying her hands on the table, fingers splayed in mild exasperation, Kate was at a loss. "What else is there to say? I told you more than you ever wanted to know about the island and its creatures days ago. And now, its most interesting character."

"There's one you left out." He took her hand again, lacing his fingers through hers, folding their palms together until he felt the softness of hers against the rough calluses of his. "The most intriguing of all, Kate Gallagher."

For the second time, Kate hadn't withdrawn from his touch.

"There's nothing to tell."

"Please."

"You asked for it." She'd meant to refuse, but once again she couldn't. "I'm thirty-three, a spinster, and an only child with no place to call home. My father was a roving ambassador who took my mother and me everywhere. We moved so often, I was a lonely, gawky child who turned to her studies and music. When I was fifteen and the gawkiness went away, I lived in Spain and modeled professionally for a Spanish designer. At seventeen I left for college to study music, but turned to law. It was then my parents were killed in a two-day coup in a country that no longer exists."

She'd begun like a schoolgirl delivering an assigned recitation in a bored chant. With the last, her voice broke. Drawing a shaky breath, she stopped. Devlin waited patiently, certain sympathy was the last thing she wanted or should have to face.

In time, with a lift of her chin, she began again. "After law school, I turned to mediation." At a loss about how to explain away the secret years in The Black Watch, or the partnership with Paul Bryce, she evaded and simplified. "For years that's what I did. Mediation in one form or another, in one place or another. Finally, I suppose I burned out.

"Now, I'm here, biding my time." *With the painful memory of Paul.* She'd looked away from Devlin, now she turned back. "And that's it, Devlin. The life of Kate Gallagher in a nutshell."

She'd done a good job of reducing thirty-three years to the bare essentials, Devlin mused. The uninformed would never guess of her service in The Black Watch, or believe a woman so lovely could survive and excel in the rigorous training required of its agents.

Only a fool wouldn't see the hurt in her. But who could understand the danger that had been her life? Or the bond of trust and love between partners. A bond obliterated, not just by separation, but by assassination and sacrifice.

To say Kate was hurting was like saying a severed hand was a laceration. He'd watched the folk of Belle Terre give the woman and her grief a wide berth. Because they couldn't know.

But Devlin knew and he understood, if only in part, that it was more than loyalty to the sworn secrecy of The Black Watch that kept her from speaking of the death of her partner. More than grief that ripped her apart.

Kate kept a painful secret hidden deeply within her grief. He knew that much, but only that. Until she trusted him enough to explain, he couldn't comfort her. He didn't know how. Instead he offered her the panacea of work.

"If you aren't in a rush to get back to Sea Watch, would you mind lending a hand?" Drawing the bandanna from his pocket, he added persuasion to the request. "Setting and nailing the railings will go much faster with someone to steady them."

"Give me a minute to pack the remnants of lunch away, and I'll join you." Opening the basket jogged her memory.

Taking out a packet of coffee, she set it on the table. "A replacement."

"This wasn't necessary, Kate. I found a cache in the freezer. But I wouldn't have died for the lack if I hadn't."

Nor would she, Kate knew, except that it kept the constant band of tension at her temples from progressing to the blurred distortions of migraines. When it happened, most were strange, and peculiarly painless. But there were others that were relentless agony, an ice pick of pain in the center of her brain. Rare, thank God. But not so rare she didn't live in fear of them.

There were medicines for migraines. Some she couldn't tolerate, with side effects worse than the ache. Others, inexplicably, were ineffective. Thus, caffeine had become her ally.

Simon's battery of physicians and psychologists suggested strongly that the best cure would be coming to terms with Paul's death. To accept his sacrifice for what it was, be grateful, and go on with her life as he would have wanted.

Kate had seen their unanimous decision as a diagnosis of weakness instead. Never one for mincing words, in one of his famous five point—five fingers folding into a fist—lectures, Simon insisted her difficulty was exactly the opposite. Difficulty, he'd reiterated adamantly, not infirmity or disorder. One every agent of The Black Watch encountered eventually. The toll of living in constant danger. The horrendous cost of strength.

Simon's theory made no sense then. It made none she wanted to face now. So, while headaches threatened she subsisted on coffee.

"You've been back to town, have you, Kate?"

As he disrupted her musing, he tied the bandanna across his forehead. Its brilliant red pattern, creating a marked contrast with his skin and hair, drew her gaze to his like a magnet. To eyes like the sky at twilight, deep, rich blue, glittering with the remnants of the light of day, but with the lurking shadows of darkness. Watching her intently, as if he sensed the restlessness and concern that had drawn her to him, he waited patiently.

For something to do, she tucked the last of the food away and closed the basket before answering. "I was there this morning."

"How was Tessa?" In his mind, the child would be as much the drawing card as the supplies Kate needed. Noticing the start of a disappointed frown, he asked, "You did see her, didn't you?"

There it was, the question she anticipated. The crux of which was none of her business, and none of her concern. Or so she'd told herself all morning.

"She wasn't there," Kate answered after a slight hesitation. "Neither was her grandmother. No one was selling flowers up front."

"Where do you suppose they were? When will they be back?"

"I spoke with the manager, thinking it might be because of the early hour. But he explained that the woman always came early, that she might miss one day, even two or three, but certainly never a week during this season."

He'd finished with the bandanna and stood attentively, one hand by his side, the other hooked at the waist of his jeans. A casual stance, belying the stirrings of disquiet. "Now she has?"

"She hasn't been back since Tessa gave me the flowers." Kate recalled the day, the flowers, the angelic child. "Granted, the manager said the old woman's days at the store were dependent on the weather and her flowers."

"She grows her own?" From the look of her, Devlin wouldn't have thought she was physically capable of tending flowers and the needs of a small child.

"Apparently. I'm not a regular at Ravenel's, but I've seen her there before." To her shame, Kate realized that in her self-absorption, she'd never stopped to buy flowers, or even to speak. "I'd seen her," she amended, "yet hardly noticed her. Until Tessa."

"Then Tessa hadn't been coming with her long?" Devlin watched the look of guilt settle over Kate's features. The look of one awakening to the needs of others. Because of the gift of a little girl, Kate Gallagher had taken one small step out of her shell, and back into the world of the living. Even better, back into the world of caring. A small step, a hopeful beginning.

"According to the manager, only for a short time."

"Then the child is visiting. I suppose, with her parents."

"That's what I assumed, at first, but the manager believes there's just the two of them. He was concerned, for he felt the old woman wasn't as well as usual last time." Thinking back, Kate recalled the tremor in the hoarse voice, the bluish tint of bloated features. Legs so grossly swollen, her ankles spilled over the tops of sensible shoes.

"Maybe that's why Tessa was with her. As grandmother's helper, to do the legwork." Devlin offered the logical explanation, but he saw Kate took no comfort in his logic. "Hey." Touching her face, lifting her chin with a knuckle against the softest of flesh, he offered the best alternative he could. "Maybe there's no reason for anyone to fret. They could just be having too much fun together to bother selling bouquets in a grocery."

"You think?"

"What I think—" he smiled to soften the warning as his fingers unfurled to cradle her cheek "—is that you're borrowing trouble. But, if it will ease your mind, I'll check by the store on my way into the lumberyard in the morning."

"Would you?" Kate wanted to catch his hand in hers,

keeping the comfort of his touch, if only for this moment. Instead she stood as she was, waiting for his answer with hope in her eyes.

"Sure." The single word was low, and deep, and infinitely gentle. "I liked the little tyke. She's a sweet kid, and one day, she's going to be a heartbreaker." Like the woman before him. The woman with hair the same color, and matching eyes. The woman who might, one day, have a daughter exactly like Tessa.

Catching a curl drifting against her cheek in the barely discernible breeze, he tucked it behind her ear. "And now, little darlin', I'd best get on with the job, or I won't need new supplies from the mainland tomorrow."

Easing back, putting a safer distance between them, he unbuttoned his sleeves and turned them back. He didn't belabor his need to return to work, nor repeat his request for help. Instead he smiled his half smile, dipped his head in a small salute, saying, "Thanks, darlin', after a morning of carpentry nothing is quite as pleasant as lunch shared with a beautiful lady."

Another salute, this time in a touch of his fingers to the bandanna, then he strolled away, a man ready to work. He'd reached the stack of lumber before she sighed softly and followed.

Kate wasn't sure why she'd come, but if it was in hopes of a distraction the paperback novel hadn't provided, coming to him had been the right choice. The beach was a beginning, for walking the sand, feeling the wind on her face and in her hair, eased the troubles caught in the cobwebs of her mind. Where the beach left off, Devlin had begun. Intriguing, kind, wounded Devlin.

Devlin, who peppered his conversations with sweet and silly names. Lady Golden Eyes, to make her want to laugh and blush at once. Darlin', in that low, slow drawl that set her heart pounding a little harder, a little faster. She'd never expected to laugh, or care, or have a friend again, but that was before Devlin, master of distraction, master tease.

The guilt for daring to feel, or to enjoy an attractive man's company, would come later. She would deal with it as she always dealt with guilt. But for now, there was a dock to be repaired, and a beguiling carpenter who needed a helping hand.

Halfway to the river, Kate became conscious of the gusto in her step and the smile on her lips. She'd reached for a smoothly planed board, lending her strength to his, when she realized the ever-present pressure at her temples wasn't there.

When he stopped in midmotion, murmuring his thanks, she answered truthfully, "My pleasure."

As she turned away for another board, she didn't see Devlin pause and frown, wondering how many hours of night music would serve as penance for daring to feel, to care, and for taking this little pleasure from it.

"How many, Kate?" he asked on a silent breath. "And for how long?"

Four

———

Kate rose to the growling roll of thunder. The bedside clock had read 5:59 as she wandered into the great room, but the world beyond the bank of windows was as dark as midnight. Low-lying clouds seethed against the horizon and, churned by the wind that drove a fast-moving storm, a dark sea mirrored the chaos of the sky. In that chaos, borne on the turning tide, racing whitecaps crested into great curling monsters bludgeoning the shore.

As wave after wave inched farther inland, Kate knew that soon the narrow road traversing the island would be under water. Little more than a shell-covered trail, the impractical concession to the ecology of the island was never meant to bear more than the sparse traffic needed for access to each home. And originally never meant to last longer than each season as it wound past carefully tended property fronts and along the base of dunes.

Since most of the traffic between town houses and island

houses transpired by boat, with many of the businesses in town enticing summer trade by providing dock space and services, that left only maintenance and rare incidents requiring the illusory road. Rather than allow asphalt or macadam on the island for that rarity, with McGregor the local king of asphalt at its helm, the owners elected to share the cost of rebuilding the meandering and natural version of an island thoroughfare whenever need be.

Granted, along with the warning that washouts were possible, Jericho had also noted they rarely occurred. In fact, at the time of her arrival, he'd assured Kate that not once in his tenure as sheriff had the tide risen so high or been so rough that the pretty path needed more than the occasional bald spot repaired.

Ordinarily, beyond the ecological damage the raging tide might inflict, Kate wouldn't care. She was well stocked, and thus content to accept the island as it was. Ready, for the sake of preserving privacy, to deal with its idiosyncrasies as they evolved. But this day was different. At this moment she would have sacrificed the naturalness, the beauty, the privacy for a dependable passage off the island. For today was the day Devlin was to pick up supplies at the lumberyard later. And, if he remembered, check at Ravenel's for Tessa and her grandmother.

Drawing the favorite orange overshirt closely about her, Kate looked into the hovering snarl of fury. With every second the tide was running faster, each wave breaking over the one before, devouring it, adding the destructive power of one to another.

Lightning slashed across the sky, turning murky clouds into wonders of fire and light. As if its rage exploded, thunder roared anew. And even as the light dimmed, and the crash of wrath quieted, the first of the pelting rain began. Sweeping from the sea in gusting sheets it battered towering windows with sand and salt and water. Raindrops cracked against glass like fistfuls of stones thrown by a mischievous hand. An ominous sign.

Even if the road remained intact, a violent downpour combined with a rising, wind-driven tide assured temporary flooding. And the loss of electricity. As always with any storm, the telephone was already lost. But none of that disturbed Kate as much as another day without news of Tessa and the old lady. News she'd been promised. If the storm hadn't come. And if memory served.

But he wouldn't have forgotten. Not Devlin.

Leaving the window, with the familiar band of pressure settling at her temples, Kate crossed to the kitchen alcove. Rising on tiptoe, she was taking down a cup when a sharp rap sounded at the back door. Glancing at the rain-swept shore, guessing who would brave the weather but wondering why, she hurried to answer.

"Devlin!"

"Morning, darlin'." Sweeping an Australian cattleman's hat from his head, he shook collected rain from the brim and, without waiting for an invitation, stepped inside. Halting by the door, he didn't venture past the mat lying by the threshold. "Some storm, huh? The tide must be ten feet above normal."

"Good heavens! What are you doing out in this?" Kate had to raise her voice to be heard over the roar of a sudden cloudburst hammering the tin roof. "Surely you aren't going into town!"

"Surely I am. And so are you."

Though pitch-black had given way to leaden gray, visibility was nearly zero. Negotiating even the best of avenues in the storm would be nearly impossible. "You're joking."

"It's just a little rain, with the worst sure to end soon." Chuckling, turning his hat in both hands, then folding it into one, he said, "Lord knows, I'm sweet enough to melt, but I never have.'' Reaching out he touched her cheek, letting his fingertips trail drown her throat to the hollow at its base. ''You might, darlin','' he teased. ''But I'll take care that you don't.''

''That won't be a problem.'' Backing away from his touch, she found the heady, rain-washed scent that clung to him followed. Anxious as she'd been about Tessa, the thought of spending time with Devlin in the close quarters of the cab of a truck, sealed away from the rest of the world by the elements, was alarming. ''Rain or no rain, I'm not going anywhere. I have things to do.''

''What things will you do?'' With most of the rain he'd brought in with him dripped off his slicker and soaked into the mat, he closed the distance between them. ''What can you do, especially when the electricity goes out like the telephone. As I'm told it's prone to do with less provocation than this little old shower.''

Kate moved back another step, beyond his reach and the possibility of another teasing touch. A touch that still lingered on her flesh like a sweet memory. To her dismay, he followed. And in her dismay she didn't realize the gale had stalled and quieted. The calm within a storm gathering strength for more.

''What will you do, Kate? Play through the day as well as the night? Wreak havoc on the piano, fretting over Tessa and the old lady, when we could be seeking the answers you want.''

He was so close now, so near. Only a long rising breath and their bodies would touch. The softness of her breasts brushing the hard plane of his chest... Kate closed her eyes and clenched her fists between them, willing the rest of the image to be gone. Tessa, she must think about Tessa. And Paul. Not Devlin.

But how could she not think of Devlin when he was so close, so beguiling. Letting her lashes lift like a fluttering veil, she met the look that searched her face intensely. "You were going to the mainland about Tessa, but also for me, weren't you?"

Folding his hands over hers, keeping the wedge of their conjoined arms as a buffer between them, with a dip of his head he brushed his lips over her knuckles. "I'm going." Straightening to meet her golden gaze again, speaking so softly the words were almost lost in the storm, he said, "But for all of us."

He was going for Tessa because a sixth sense that saved him more times than he could count, and had failed him only once, warned that the child needed someone. He was going for Kate because he had seen the hope of her salvation in an enchanting smile of gratitude for a bouquet of flowers. He was going for himself. He knew now, in some inexplicable way, his own survival was tied with Kate's.

"Where would you find these answers?" Kate left her hands in his. Accepting the power that was comforting and exciting.

"After the lumberyard, we go to Ravenel's." He spoke in terms of both of them, for he was sure she would go.

"And if they aren't there?"

"Then we go to Jericho."

"You think he'll know about the woman? And Tessa?"

"If anyone can help us, Jericho can. If he doesn't have the answers we want, he'll know where we can find them."

Kate had met the sheriff only rarely, and briefly. What she knew of the man was more by reputation than personal experience. But he had called Devlin a friend and a good man. Judging from Devlin's confidence in Jericho, the feeling was mutual.

Kate's service in The Black Watch had taught her to err on the side of caution when dealing with figures of au-

thority. *Especially* figures of authority. In the field, and on
assignment, she seldom accepted any judgment but her
own. The self-reliance had kept her alive. Along with Paul
Bryce. But Belle Terre wasn't the field, Tessa wasn't an
assignment. And this was Devlin.

"All right, Devlin." As easily and trusting as that, her
decision was made. In the dark slicker and dark hat, he'd
loomed larger than life in the whipping rain. Seeing him
like this, calmly braving the elements, taking the furor in
his easy stride, Kate knew she hadn't been wrong in thinking much of his life had been spent chasing adventure,
courting danger. An autumn squall, even one shaping into
epic proportions, would be just another challenge.

In a battle of wits, man pitting strength and knowledge
against the elements, Kate chose Devlin. "When should
we leave?"

"As soon as you can be ready." There was no question,
no smug victory. Only a calm acceptance, and a look of
relief.

An instinctive but unneeded glance at the window
showed little hope for immediate improvement in the
weather. By now he'd recognized a pattern. If ever the
storm eased back, it was only to follow the vacillating
tenor with a formidable gain of force. "Quickly, before
the road to the bridge floods, if you can."

"I can." Stepping away from him, away from the circle
of his scent, away from his touch, Kate swiftly took stock
of the little that must be done before leaving the house to
the mercies of the storm. "There's a book with a list of
instructions the owner left for me to follow in case of a
hurricane."

"Get it for me." The storm didn't qualify as a hurricane
in either scope or power. But that didn't mean this rogue
would do any less damage. If fact, Devlin knew from experience, the rogue could be worse. Short, quick, deadly,

and destructive. "I'll see to what should be done while you change."

Wasting neither words nor time, Kate went directly to the book of detailed, hand-written instruction. She didn't insult him by explaining as she passed it to him. "Ten minutes, tops."

"That's a promise?"

The wind surged, the house shook on its pilings, dishes chattered in cabinets. The top of a palmetto tree snapped like a twig and tumbled across the roof screeching like chalk against slate. Kate had vacationed on beaches around the world, yet never lived near the sea for any length. But it didn't require being a veteran to know the time frame for negotiating the shell road was limited. "Ten isn't a promise, but seven is."

"And you keep your promises." Devlin's voice was sure.

"As you do, my friend." Kate didn't wait to see the effect, if any, of her spoken trust. She'd promised seven minutes, seven it would be. Hurrying away, believing implicitly that he would see to the precautions on the list, her mind was already sifting through her closet, deciding what was practical for a deluge.

Jeans and a denim shirt, and because the storm brought a chill, a bulky sweatshirt. Waterproof hiking boots, a cap tucked in her hip pocket. A glide of lip gloss, a whisk of mascara for her eyes—because she couldn't risk more than these small vanities—then she tackled the tangles in her hair. Surprisingly, it cooperated, presenting not one stubborn snarl. Once it was banded tightly at her nape, she had a minute to spare, to catch her breath.

Contemplating herself in the mirror, she realized she was stroking her hand, and the knuckles Devlin had kissed.

His hands were hard, strong, work-worn. His lips were soft and tender. And it meant nothing. Except that he was a thoughtful, compassionate man. Perhaps, because of his own mysterious hurt, more compassionate than anyone she'd met in all her life.

"Just part of the charm, Lady Golden Eyes." Kate met her gaze sternly in the mirror. "It meant nothing." Nothing but a token of a friendship that for all its newness went deeper than any she'd experienced. In a tone as stern as her look she drove the point home, "Friendship, that's all it was, and all I want."

Leaving the dressing table, tugging the cap from her pocket, she settled it at an angle over her forehead. She was ready. Ready for Devlin, the friend she'd never had, with a minute to spare.

The drive into Belle Terre was not as Kate expected. The gray day took on a subtle beauty, with mists rising and swirling and gathering about roofs and treetops between each drenching. The little road stood undamaged for a while yet. If there were treacherous patches, Devlin's skill at the wheel smoothed them out.

The bridge that joined the island to the mainland arched over the fog-shrouded land like a bridge beginning and ending in nothing. But in her trust that he would keep them on safe and firm ground, she even relaxed and enjoyed the mystic look of sights so familiar. Even Hobie's gatehouse looked more like a fantasy than the domain of a no-nonsense guardian of a small corner of paradise.

"I wonder where he is."

Devlin looked up from his concentrated negotiation of the downward arch of the bridge. "Hobie?"

"He wasn't in his house." She didn't pass through the gates often, but when she did, he was always there to send her through with a cheerful wave. "Do you suppose something's wrong?"

"I don't know what could be. Since it's an unlikely day

for intruders, he probably took a few minutes away from his post." In a glance away from the road he saw her troubled face. "Hey." His hand curved around her shoulder, his palm cupping the sharp bones as his fingers stroked taut muscles. "Tell you what, if Hobie isn't back at his post when we return, we'll stop and check. Deal?"

He didn't take his hand away until she clasped her own hands tightly in her lap and nodded once.

"That's my darlin'. A worrywart, but a kindhearted lady."

Neither spoke again until he drew the truck to a halt before the lumberyard. The rain had slowed, falling sporadically and in patches. When she started to leave the cab, he stopped her with another touch. "Wait here, this won't take a minute." Fishing a folded paper from a pocket, he flipped it with a finger. "I've itemized the materials I need to finish the dock. To save the road, I'm going to ask that they be delivered by boat."

He was out of the truck McGregor kept for emergencies, and striding through a light shower before Kate could agree or disagree. She watched the familiar figure disappear through massive doors. Then she was alone with the morass of her thoughts, wondering what she would do if today brought no word of Tessa. Why should she care? What about the little girl and her gift of flowers touched her so deeply, leaving an indelible memory?

"Just as I promised, not long." Devlin swung into the truck, filling the small space with his presence again. Turning the key in the ignition, he let the motor idle. "Listen," he began hesitantly, "why don't you let me check with the grocer?"

"You mean, I should wait in the truck again."

"Yeah." His head dipped once in a nod. "I do."

"But what if she's there?" Correcting herself, Kate amended, "What if they're both there?"

Devlin said nothing. Nor did he turn from the misty view.

"You don't think either will be. Today, or ever." Kate laid a hand on his wrist, drawing his gaze to her. "Do you, Devlin?"

He was slow in answering, his reluctance apparent. "No, Kate, I don't."

"Can you tell me why?"

Covering her hand with his, he moved his fingers restively over hers. "I can't explain. Call it instinct, gut feeling. One of those things that twists inside like a dull knife."

"Then you think there's trouble."

"Kate." He crushed her hand in his, forgetting for a moment that her fragile bones were no match for his strength. "Sweetheart, I don't know. Except this doesn't feel good."

"Do you want to go back home? Back to the island?"

"No. That wouldn't solve anything." Releasing her, he watched as she drew her hand away, then reached for the gear. "Maybe it's just the weather, and the gloom is contagious."

And maybe it was that he was afraid she would be hurt in this first venture into feeling again, and caring. The first step back into the real world. If this went wrong, would there ever be a second step, or any world for her at all beyond the life of a recluse and the crashing echoes of tortured night music?

He'd hoped to spare her, but he couldn't. "We don't need to check by the grocer's. The old lady isn't there. Neither is Tessa."

"Not there?" Large golden eyes stared at him beneath the fan of darkened lashes. "How do you know?"

"I called the store."

"From the island? If you already knew, why did we come to the mainland?"

His fingers curled around the steering wheel. He'd looked away, staring though the windshield at rivulets trickling down the glass, but now he turned to her. "I couldn't call from the island, the telephone lines were already out. Remember? It's likely they'll be out in town soon, but not yet."

Kate knew then part of the time he'd spent in Building Supply had been for the call. "So, what next? Jericho?"

"Seemed like a good idea before." The gears of McGregor's ancient truck scraped and complained as Devlin shifted into reverse. "Seems like it now."

A matronly clerk with steel-framed glasses perched on her long nose glared over a sheaf of papers as Devlin escorted Kate into the anteroom of the sheriff's office. One look at the unwelcoming disposition and Kate expected to be told to wipe her feet, don't drip on the carpet, or just go away.

"May I help you?" If words could frost, these would have.

"Uh-oh," Devlin muttered in Kate's ear as he walked with her to a seat. "Looks like someone's a tad disturbed."

"More than a tad," Kate agreed in a tone as low. "If our welcome is any indication, I don't think we'll be seeing Jericho."

"Maybe not." He glanced over his shoulder and back at Kate. "But we didn't come through this storm just to leave at the first obstacle. Sit tight, let me talk to the watchdog for a minute."

"Talk to her? About what, Devlin?"

"At the moment, darlin', I haven't a clue." With a lift of a brow and a half smile, he sauntered to the desk cheerfully, as if their greeting had been pleasant.

Kate heard the low, slow, drawling, "Mornin', ma'am."

She saw the haughty look, with penciled eyebrows reaching toward a graying hairline. She heard a second greeting even frostier than the first. Then Devlin's voice dipped, grew softer. After a time, the cold responses grew softer, as well. And finally warmer.

Once, Devlin leaned on the desk, his hands braced on the edge, and he smiled down at the lady, whose name tag read Molly O'Brian. Then, wonder of wonders, Devlin chuckled, and a blush crept over Officer O'Brian's face, the color leavening the harsh cast of her features, making her almost pretty.

"He left strict orders that he wasn't to be disturbed, barring an emergency, but, for you, I'll check." Officer O'Brian slid back her chair and stood, a smile shaping lips that once were frozen in a grim line.

As she turned to go, Devlin caught her hand. "Thank you, I appreciate the trouble." Releasing her, he touched her cheek. "You know, Officer O, you should smile more often. A smile from a pretty lady makes the world a better place for the rest of us."

"Ha!" The eyebrows lifted again, this time over dancing eyes. "O'Hara, you've kissed the blarney stone one time too many."

Devlin shrugged and smiled. "Maybe so." His voice dropped again, intimately. "But it didn't make me a liar."

Molly O'Brian was actually laughing as she walked down the hall to Jericho Rivers's office, and disappeared inside.

Kate waited until he faced her to comment. "Neatly done. You got what you wanted, and made her day in the process."

"A better day, I hope."

Kate didn't doubt that he meant it. He truly wanted Officer O'Brian to be happier. Not just to get the concessions he sought, but for herself. "Considering the lovely blush, I'd bet on it."

"It was, wasn't it? Lovely, I mean."

Kate grew thoughtful, a nebulous impression left by the encounter clicked into place. Devlin O'Hara was a man who loved women, honestly, in every shape, every form, and of every age. *And we love him right back.*

"O'Hara, Miss Gallagher." Molly O'Brian stood by her desk, the blush faded but the pleasant expression still intact. "Sheriff Rivers will see you now."

Kate stood quickly, grateful for a change in the direction of her thoughts. Still preoccupied by this insight into Devlin, she expressed the necessary gratitude and pleasantries to Officer O'Brian by rote, then found herself immediately in Sheriff Jericho Rivers's private office.

"Kate." Tossing a letter aside, Jericho left his seat and circled his desk to take both her hands in his. "It's been a while since I've seen you. But from the look of you, I must say island life certainly agrees with you."

Kate spoke her thanks graciously as the sheriff released her to greet Devlin with a strong, silent handshake. As with the best of friends and men of a breed, the dark and striking men seemed to communicate more with a look and a commanding grasp than with a thousand words. Or any words.

Yet in this encounter, witnessing the exchange, Kate was startled by the realization that in their few brief conversations she'd learned more about Belle Terre's respected sheriff than she'd learned in days from her fellow islander.

Jericho was the larger of the two, a Goliath of a man with the mark of his mixed ancestry evident in the ruggedness of his features. Part Scot, part French, with a trace of American Indian, he'd told her in their first brief meeting. The latter especially not surprising, given the dark skin, darker straight hair, the steady and somber air of utter calm.

From the occasional but rare gossip she couldn't escape while attending errands in town, she'd gleaned that Jericho was the scion of the town's most prominent family. That he'd been a star high school and college athlete, and a merit scholar. After a few years as quarterback in professional football a severe injury had ended his career. Turning away numerous offers from prestigious law firms, he'd put his law degree in mothballs in favor of returning home to Belle Terre to wear the sheriff's badge.

Speculations about the gold band he wore on his right hand ran rife. But not even the most knowledgeable gossip had an answer.

There it was, virtually Jericho's life story. But what did she know of Devlin beyond that the features he shared with Jericho were, she assumed from his name, Irish. She'd deduced from the half smile and the look in his solemn eyes that there had been problems in his life. She'd guessed that he'd been an adventurer.

Deducing, guessing, and assuming aside, beyond the face-value observance that he was kind, compassionate, and a man who cared for and respected women deeply, what did she really know?

Devlin did not seem a reticent man by nature. Was the difficulty that had driven him to seek refuge on the island so great? Or was his silence deliberate?

The startling notion brought her attention sharply to the men finishing their friendly exchange. Bells were going off. Little scraps of gossip even an organization as clandestine as The Watch couldn't squelch were remembered. Rivers and O'Hara, the names had been linked before. But not Devlin O'Hara. Kieran!

Kieran O'Hara, known as the Nomad within The Black

Watch. Brother of the legendary Valentina O'Hara Courtenay, retired from the same organization.

Kate and Paul had worked with Kieran. Kieran, with dark skin, dark hair, eyes like the sky reflected in a mountain lake.

Were the looks and the name a coincidence? Or stretching coincidence too far? Much too far?

"Kate." With an outstretched hand, Devlin drew her into the circle of conversation.

Avoiding his touch, not daring to meet his gaze, she stepped to a chair opposite the one he was offering.

Once they were seated, Jericho had returned to his seat, and was first to speak into an awkward silence. "Now, how can I help you? What's so important it coaxed two recluses to the mainland in the midst of the season's worst storm?"

"I think the lady can tell it best." A puzzled expression on his face, Devlin deferred to her. "Kate."

Drawing a breath, she began. "The older lady who sells flowers at Ravenel's..." Jericho didn't speak, and Kate continued, "The manager says she's normally there most every day. But now she's been missing for some time. By missing, I mean not at the store. She didn't look well last time and there was a little girl."

"You're concerned, but you don't know her name?"

"To my everlasting shame, no, Jericho."

Hearing the tremble in her voice, the sheriff sighed, knowing he must tell this troubled young woman the worst. "Her name was Mary Sanchez. She came to Belle Terre a few years ago. In those years, she lived very quietly down by the east end of the river on a little flower farm she called Mary's Garden."

"Her name *was?* She *lived?*" Kate repeated. "Past tense."

"Mary died two days ago."

As Jericho's words fell like a stone between them, Devlin wanted to reach out to Kate. He ached to comfort her. But the coldness that emanated from her shut him out.

"Two days ago?" she repeated. "So suddenly?"

"Not so suddenly." Jericho might not know all his charges, but he would know someone as visible as Mary Sanchez. "She'd been ill for a long time, a failing heart finally failed completely."

Kate made no sound beyond a broken sob, for a woman she didn't know. A woman who had given her flowers. Flowers from Tessa, who hoped she wouldn't look so sad.

A ceiling fan Devlin hadn't noticed stirred the cloying air and teased an errant curl against Kate's pale cheek. Resisting a need to touch her, knowing instinctively yet not understanding why his touch had suddenly become unwelcome, he turned to Jericho. "And the little girl?" he asked softly. "Mary called her Tessa."

"She's with family. Mary had time to see to that, at least."

"Where? How do you know?"

The question was Devlin's, but Jericho addressed his reply to Kate. "At first, Mary told her neighbors Tessa was visiting while her parents worked through a bad patch in their marriage. When her health took a drastic turn, she admitted there was no marriage and only one parent. Tessa's mother, who was terminally ill."

"Why two stories?" Kate asked. "Why not tell the truth?"

"Because Mary knew she didn't have long herself. She confided in the same neighbor that she was fearful that if Tessa's situation and her poor health were discovered, social services would take the child." Jericho raked a hand over strained features. "Mary didn't want Tessa caught up in the system. Instead, she hinted at other arrangements, and a secret, distant relative."

"Then you don't know who this relative is?" Devlin asked.

Jericho nodded. "Mary would never say."

"Why?" Kate wondered aloud. "Why would a name matter?"

"We won't know that until we find the relative and Tessa." Jericho's fist clenched. "We will find them, Kate."

"How can you be sure any of this is true? Is Tessa's mother really dying? Has she died? Does this secret relative exist?" Devlin had barely taken his eyes from Kate, until now, as he addressed Jericho. "What proof do you have of any of this?"

"Mary, and the woman she was, is my proof. Mary, and an unusual event." Jericho paused, but didn't keep them waiting long. "The day before she died, Mary left her house with Tessa. When she returned, she was alone. I believe that in her last hours, she left the child in trusted hands."

"She managed all that, before she went into the hospital?" Kate believed as Jericho, and marveled at Mary's determination.

"Mary died in her greenhouse. A neighbor found her."

"Then, surely this person has come forward."

Concerned, Jericho looked from Kate to Devlin, weighing his answer, he turned back to Kate. "I'm afraid not. And there's no family on record. No one who would've been Tessa's mother. No mystery relative."

"No one came to the services?" Kate grieved for a lonely woman who died as she lived. Alone.

"Only neighbors and friends. She was cremated," Jericho said. "As late as last night no one had claimed her ashes."

"Have you looked for Tessa?" Kate asked in an undertone.

"We've looked. We'll look until we exhaust every avenue." Jericho didn't explain that there were no avenues, no pictures, no records. The little girl called Tessa had vanished.

"We have to keep in mind that Mary would see the little one had the best of care. Trust in that, Kate. It will help you sleep at night." Pausing, Jericho Rivers, sheriff of Belle Terre, added, "Until the day we find her."

"Until that day," Devlin said as softly as he stood, bringing the interview to an end. The storm had passed, the rain stopped, but he knew the drive to the island would be troubled.

Five

Standing a pace behind Kate, Devlin was in a quandary, wondering what he could say to her in this mercurial mood.

He expected her disappointment over Tessa. He shared her grief for Mary. But this consuming distraction that had grown deeper and more puzzling with every mile home was more than disappointment. Even more than grief. Something neither Jericho's belief and assurance the little girl was in good hands nor finding Hobie in his customary place could placate.

After the elderly Hobie, with his crippled back and always immaculate uniform, waved them through the gate and across the bridge to the island, Devlin hoped Kate's mood would brighten. For each person there was a haven, a refuge from troubles and troubled times. Before Joy, before he'd lost the privilege, his haven had been his family, his refuge the Chesapeake. Perhaps because her nomadic life had been more rootless than his, Kate had no real place to call home. And, in a little-known conflict, in a tiny, little-known Middle Eastern country, disaster had taken the anchor of family from her.

Cast adrift, she'd lived her life alone, without the security even the strongest must seek now and again. No, Devlin amended vehemently, Kate lived and survived without the security *especially* the strong must have. The place and people with whom the mavericks could simply be, without judgment, or condemnation.

That singular place where the wounded warrior could heal in mind, and spirit, and heart. He'd come to believe that Summer Island could be that place for Kate. A healing place instead of a hiding place. He believed it now, hoping the return to Summer Island would be a return to peace and sanctuary.

He'd sensed the subtle change in her while speaking with Jericho. Once away from the sheriff's office, though silent, the journey from the mainland had begun easily enough. In tandem with her darkening mood, the passage deteriorated into a series of stalls and starts before the truck crossed the city boundary. Beneath a sky washed clean of all vestiges of clouds or storm, the sodden road was a morass of washed-out pavement, slippery puddles, and broken tree limbs lying like barriers across the winding way.

The road crews were already working, with chain saws and warning signs in hand. Next would come linemen for power and telephone companies. Help going first to the greater population. With few in residence on the barrier islands, it would be some time before either electric or telephone service was restored to them.

Along with its raging clamor, the dissipated storm had taken every breath of wind with it, turning cool air sultry and dead calm. In it every soundless moment reverberated,

drawing silence into itself, closing them in disparate co-
coons within the cab of the truck. Devlin was relieved
when he drove through the drenched and dripping tunnel
of live oaks. An end signaling the beginning of the lush
tropical causeway leading to the island.

Hobie in place and smiling was a positive sign. That the
shell road still snaked among the dunes, heavily damaged
and in need of serious repair but passable, was the second.
And the last.

Devlin drove directly to Sea Watch. Drawing to a stop
beneath the pillared structure, he intended to escort her into
the house, but Kate was out of the truck and halfway up
the stairs before he could reach her. At the door, his hand
closed over hers, taking the key. As she relinquished it
without a word, he found himself wishing she would resist,
or argue. Insist she was a modern independent woman capable of unlocking her own door. Anything to draw her
from the frame of mind that absorbed her.

Instead she'd waited while he dealt with the lock, then
stepped past him through the open door. Without bothering
to ask him in, or send him away, she moved to the middle
of the room and stopped, as if she didn't know where to
go, or what to do next.

Though the storm had ended, with the sun sliding toward the back of the house away from the bank of windows, the room lay in shadow. Beyond the deck, sea and
sky melded into one, with no beginning and no end. A
stunning illusion. A gift of the storm.

But Kate didn't notice even as she moved to the glass,
her arms hugging her sides as if she were cold in the close,
humid air. Caught between the glare of the windows and
the twilight of the room, she was a stark shadow as black
as her mood. What could he say? Devlin wondered. What
could he do, when he didn't understand?

This was not completely about Tessa. That much he

knew instinctively, with a surety he couldn't explain, and wouldn't try. But, perhaps Tessa would be the place to start.

"Kate," he began, then fell silent for an instant when she tensed as if her name from his tongue was a whip scoring her tender flesh. Forcing patience, he waited for something, some reaction. There was nothing. Beyond the single move, she was a still and silent specter. Devlin O'Hara, the cocksure and glib-of-tongue before Joy Bohannon and now Kate Gallagher, was at a loss for words.

The right words. For Kate he must have the right words, make the right decision. He'd failed once, he mustn't again.

"Kate. Sweetheart." In his own distress, he was not aware of an endearment he rarely used, or that the teasing lilt that accompanied them was absent. "She's okay. Jericho's comfortable with this, he trusts Mary Sanchez to have seen to her safekeeping."

"He's looking for her." Kate didn't turn or relax.

"That's just Jericho. Thorough to the end. Seeking concrete proof for what he knows in his gut." Pausing and remembering, Devlin drew a long breath. "Mary loved that child. Anyone could see that. Everyone did. I did, on a glance. I went into town today acting on a hunch Tessa needed someone. She did, but now I believe that wherever she is, she's okay. A brave lady saw to that."

"I know." The words were a nuance more than a whisper.

But they stopped him abruptly. "You know."

Raking her hands across her face, Kate pressed against her temples. "I hope he'll keep looking for Tessa. But I know he's right. I can't imagine how she managed it, being so terribly ill." Kate faltered and Devlin heard the note of melancholy, for a lost life and a lost child who touched her life for only a moment, but in that moment, irrevocably. Yet, still, there was something more.

Stepping forward, he halted by her side. "Kate, dear, kind Kate." With her name a comforting murmur, his palm curled around her throat, his thumb rested at the base of her chin, his fingers caressed her nape. "I'm sorry."

Exerting the little pressure needed to close the space between them, he brought her before him. Tossing away the cap she'd worn for the rain, he looked into the fathomless well of her gaze. A look that told him nothing. Sighing in defeat, he drew her forehead to his chest. Holding her unresponsive body close, offering his strength, he waited again for resistance that never came.

Aware of her own stamina warring against the fragility she would detest, he moved carefully. Stroking the taut muscles at the base of her neck, he found the knotted tension of worry, exhaustion, and secret sorrow. Sliding his fingers beneath the fall of her hair, he found the band that held her hair and slipped it away.

As the bright garland fell to the floor, keeping her body close to the support of his with one hand, with the other he combed the tumbling mass with his fingers. Letting each stroke glide from her nape to the burnished ends, he smoothed each strand into order.

Kate didn't respond, but she didn't resist when the hand at her waist glided over her back to her shoulders. Encouraged, folding both hands at the hollows beneath her earlobes, he let them drift to her temples. Stroking the pulsing blue-veined flesh, as he'd seen her do, he exerted the gentlest of circling pressure.

The breath she drew was a sigh, low, sweet, almost a purr. In that maddening moment, he felt the heat of her body curling into his, accepting his strength and the comfort he offered. And in that moment he wanted her as he'd never wanted a woman before.

Stunned by the power of his response, and by the fierce blaze of desire that had lain dormant for so long, his mind and body were in utter chaos. He wanted to sweep her into his arms, keeping her close, fitting soft curves to hard planes. He wanted to taste her mouth, to drink from her, taking her sweetness for his own. He wanted her heart and her soul, to have, to hold, to keep.

In all his life, he'd never wanted a woman so much. A woman he would want and need forever.

He didn't understand this depth of need and caring. He didn't know this Devlin O'Hara, this maddened man. All he knew was that it hurt when Kate shut herself away from him. Yet he understood that today, with disappointment and another loss heaped upon the morass of the past, a door that had opened a sliver shattered, leaving her raw and reeling with volatile emotions.

He'd learned from his own trials that in such times friends and enemies, and love and hate, wore strange faces. Trust was a scary proposition and a desperate need. A confusion, leaving one vulnerable. Devlin O'Hara, and even the madman he'd become, had been many things to many people, but never a seducer of vulnerable women. He wouldn't begin now.

Taking her by the shoulders, he moved her a step away. Away from the heat that consumed him. Away from the need and desire that ran rampant within him. Fiercely, he reminded himself he'd come to help, not hurt. To heal, not wound.

Leaning forward, paying penance for almost-committed sins, he brushed his lips over her forehead. ''You've had a tense and frustrating day, and it will be some time before the service crews get to our electricity or telephone.'' Stroking a strand of hair from her shoulder, because he had to touch at least that part of her, he said, ''With the surf up and the tide riding high, there's little beach for walking, so why don't you rest awhile?''

As if she were waking from a trance, Kate moved back another step. The golden gaze that had stared blankly back at him, blazed now with amber fire. ''Who are you? What are you?''

Startled, he answered warily, each word drawn out carefully. ''I've told you, I'm only Devlin O'Hara.''

''Only Devlin O'Hara.'' A brow arched, her chin lifted a challenging notch. ''And...''

From her stance and the angle of her head, he knew she would wait as long as she must for the answer. ''And most recently, I was a bush pilot, of a sort.''

Shifting deliberately, letting the light at her back turn her again into no more than a darkened shadow, Kate parroted, ''Most recently, of a sort. Which means?''

''Until five months ago, I was sole owner and pilot of a charter service in Alaska.'' Devlin was surprised to hear the words fall so calmly from his lips. He hadn't thought he could speak of Alaska and flying so dispassionately again.

Kate paced before the windows in a measured step. Turning at the last to face him again, her solemn face still half in light, half in shadow, he could imagine her before a witness stand. Or arguing her case before the intractable head of a rogue Third World country. She would have been good at her job. Perhaps too good, as witnessed by an assassin's bullet gone astray.

''A bush pilot.'' Kate interpreted succinctly, assimilating every fact and nuance of its wording. He'd abandoned a daring profession and one coast for another. Unusual. ''That covers a lot of territory, leaving a lot in between. Where in Alaska?'' The exact location might not matter, but to Kate no detail was insignificant. ''Why did you leave?''

"I lived in the town of Talkeetna, but the mountains, and especially Denali, were my livelihood." There it was, Denali, the specter that haunted his nights more than three thousand miles away.

Kate waited, guessing by the stark look in his eyes that it was more than wanderlust that influenced the coastal trek. She would hear the story, at his own pace.

"My plane went down...on the mountain." His voice was halting, remote. "After that, ferrying climbers and research teams to the summits and glaciers was never the same."

Kate didn't dismiss the emotion she heard, but filed it away for another time. "Now you're here."

Devlin nodded. This was the Ice Princess described in the dossiers of The Black Watch. In her fugue of remorse, she hadn't lost her edge. She was still magnificent in action, still indomitable, still purposeful and unswerving. When it came to cross-examination, the ice in her veins was still frosty, if not frozen.

"Here." She emphasized the word, giving it significance with tone and timbre. "Quite a long way from Alaska. Not as long from the Chesapeake, and your family." The mediator became prosecutor, playing the trump card. "The eccentric, benevolent, and wealthy O'Haras. The spectacularly gifted siblings, two of whom include Kieran and Valentina O'Hara, of The Black Watch."

Devlin stood mute, his surprise unrevealed. But, he wondered, was he really surprised? That the lady was sharp and intuitive was a forgone conclusion. Any fool who thought grief and guilt destroyed it was far worse than a fool.

"Who sent you, Devlin O'Hara? Was it Simon?" She took a step closer, keeping her face half hidden and half revealed, using the advantage that the target of her interrogation could never quite read her expression as she zeroed in for the coup de grâce. "Has he decided I'm a security risk? A loose cannon?"

A gesture toward shore encompassed the whole of the island. "Is that the reason a handsome and mysterious stranger arrived unexpectedly to share a deserted beach with the latest emotional casualty of The Black Watch?"

The Black Watch. She'd used the name deliberately. And, for proof, a second time. Devlin showed neither shock nor denial. Most telling of all, no curiosity. Few were privy to the name given a government organization so clandestine that officially it was nameless. Even among families, one member might understand that another worked for the government. But recognize the name? Never.

"Is that what today and yesterday, and all the days before were about?" Had the kindness been a lie? A ploy to gain her trust?

Kate didn't want to admit how much the idea hurt. In her outburst she'd circled the room, arms crossed, containing the disappointment. Now she dropped them by her side. Fists clenched, forgetting ingrained tactics of her profession, she faced him, letting the revealing light fall on her face. "Are you my watchdog? Here to make sure I don't commit some grave mistake in my…" She searched for words. "Shall we call it my delicate state?"

"Kate, no." Taking an instinctive step toward her, he stopped abruptly when she recoiled. "I'm not part of The Watch. I've done a few small chores for Simon, because I was in the right part of the world at the right time, or knew a key figure. But not now. Simon cares, he's concerned, but he didn't send me."

"Then why did you come?" She was rigid, flushed in her anger. The color in her cheeks offering an attractive contrast to the golden blaze of her eyes. "Surely you don't think I believe any of this, or the meeting at Ravenel's was coincidence.''

Devlin never turned his gaze from the dazzling spectacle of her fire. "I haven't lied to you, Kate. I won't now, or ever. The meeting in Ravenel's was no accident. I was there to see you."

"How? Why?" The demanding questions were bitter explosions in the sultry, shadowy room. "You didn't know I existed before this, you couldn't have. Yet you say Simon didn't send you..." Breaking off, she realized it wasn't that he might be Black Watch, or even Simon's man, but the subterfuge and false pretenses that infuriated her. That he wasn't who and what he pretended. That to Devlin, Kate Gallagher was no more than an assignment.

"To spy?" Devlin finished for her. "Never."

"I'm supposed to believe you? Just like that?" Kate paced away, then swung back, eyes blazing through the shadows, pinning him in place. "Would you believe, Devlin?"

He'd caught glimpses of the woman Valentina insisted had made her mark within The Watch as few others. He hadn't doubted Kate's abilities or expertise. Being one of Simon McKinzie's chosen was irrefutable proof. Even so, he'd taken his sister's profuse claims with a grain of reservation, considering them the product of Valentina's persuasive zeal.

Now he was witnessing the Ice Princess in no-holds-barred battle. She was astute, quick, intuitive, everything Valentina insisted. And wrong.

Wrong and magnificent. Counselor extraordinaire dressed in jeans, denim shirt, and no-nonsense hiking boots, with the discarded cap and sweatshirt lying on the sofa. Not the costume de rigueur for high court or the diplomatic round table, but more than effective in the soft light of a beach house.

That Simon might have sent a guardian was not the issue. Kate was angered by what she perceived as his deception.

He couldn't let her think that of Simon, or of him. "If you asked that I believe, yes, Kate, I would." He smiled his half smile as he held her gaze. "Just like that."

Kate was startled by the frank admission. But if he'd misrepresented himself once, he would again. "I think you should leave, Devlin. I don't want to hear any more of this."

"I think you do." Closing the distance between them, he faced her anger and the hurt of betrayal.

"No." When she would have backed away from him, he caught her shoulders. Stiffening in icy rage, she demanded fiercely, quietly, "Let me go. Then leave, and don't come back."

"Not until you hear me out."

"I said no."

Flinging her hands against his imprisoning arms, she would have broken free had he not anticipated the move. Fearful he would hurt her if she struggled, he shook her gently. "Dammit, Kate, Valentina sent me. Not Simon."

"Valentina?" Kate went still in disbelief. "She wouldn't. If your sister is the woman I've been told she is, she would have no part of this subterfuge."

Letting his hands slide down her arms, his fingers brushing over hers before slipping away, he willed her to listen, to believe. "There is no subterfuge. And it would be fairer to say Valentina asked me to come. As much for myself as for you. Hear me out, and you'll understand."

"This is ridiculous." Then Kate remembered the beautiful half smile that left the extraordinary O'Hara eyes untouched. The wicked grin with a sense of hurt lying beneath. How many times had she been convinced there was devastating sorrow hidden deeply within him? When she looked at him, how many times had she sensed a kindred wounded soul?

Recognizing doubt, Devlin chose reason. "Is it? Can you not conceive of Valentina caring enough to help?"

"She wanted to help, so she sent you?"

Devlin nodded his answer, waiting beneath her narrowed stare. Beyond the windows a day begun in storm progressed into clear, sunny late afternoon. Too bad life was never so simple, he thought. A quick fray, then done, leaving splendor in its wake.

"Why?" A puzzled note rang in the question. As with all agents, her problems were problems of The Black Watch. He wasn't one of the sector. She believed that now. Were he one of Simon's chosen, somehow, some way she would have known him, by name and reputation, if not in person. A man like Devlin would be larger than life, even among the clandestine. But believing didn't supply the answers she needed. "This concerns The Watch. Given its choices, why you?"

Abandoning wishful reflections, he touched her face, briefly tracing the curve of her chin. She didn't respond, but it was enough that she didn't recoil again. "I was Valentina's chosen," he said in parody of another name given to Simon's recruits. "In that great, compassionate heart of hers, the O'Hara family's self-appointed mother hen believes I need you, Kate. As much, if not more than you need me."

"Valentina." Kate had no brothers or sisters, nor even any cousins, or aunts, or uncles. As a little girl, while she and her mother trekked from country to country with her father, sometimes barely staying long enough to unpack, Kate had dreamed of a family. Someone to be her playmate, to share secrets. To fight, to quarrel. To care and be concerned. Even to be nosy and interfere.

She'd met Valentina face-to-face only once, but had

come away from the meeting wishing she knew this beautiful contradiction, the gentle assassin.

"You've met her," Devlin reminded.

"Once."

"But once was enough." At any other time, Devlin would have smiled imagining the first meeting with Valentina, even for one only remotely familiar with her role in The Watch.

It was enough, for as Kate knew it would have been with Devlin, Valentina's reputation preceded her. And not only Valentina's. Simon's O'Haras and their mates were legend within The Watch. Word and awe of their exploits transcended even the secrecy within the world's most clandestine organization.

Meeting Devlin's gaze, keeping it, she knew in her heart that once there had been laughter in his eyes. Laughter like blue fire, wild and free, as he had surely been before the joy in his life was snuffed out. "There's a story here," she said at last. "I think I should hear it."

Devlin agreed. Offering his hand, he waited for her touch. A sign of trust regained, until his story was told.

Nothing about him changed. There was no frown, or grimace, only a subtle unveiling nuance, perceived rather than seen, causing reflection. "You don't want to tell me, do you?"

Kate's observation was shrewd. The counselor, again, this time reading the surfacing emotions he'd kept hidden for so long. Emotions and truths he never wanted her to know, but now she must. "No. But you have to understand."

"Because…?" Looking to his open hand and back again to his face, she waited. No longer the counselor, but a woman, instead, wanting a woman's answers.

"Because I need for you to understand." After a thoughtful pause, he continued in a solemn voice. "Because when you hear what I have to say, if it's what you want, I'll leave.''

She smelled of a subtle perfume and of rain. Every breath he drew was laden with the scent, soft, delicate, enticing. He hadn't wanted to come to Summer Island. He'd never intended to stay. That had been his monotonous credo every minute of every hour, until he heard her play, filling the night with music. Now he wondered how he could bear it if she wanted him to go.

His outstretched hand was curled and waiting, and when she slipped her fingers over his palm, his clasp was strong, but gentle. With a rueful smile he led her to the sofa.

Kate's vanquished anger was replaced by a growing dilemma. One that left her torn between the need to know and the risk of losing Devlin, the friend she'd never had. Amid the steady roar of a surf still wild, in the clamor of raucous gulls quarreling over treasures the tumbling sea swept onto shifting sand, a waiting silence enveloped them. A man and a woman, hurt and hurting, but reaching out for a place of peace.

After a time of pondering, Devlin laughed a humorless laugh. ''In the wake of that less than brilliant argument, I don't know what to say, or where to begin.''

''Begin with who you are.'' Her hand was still in his, she made no effort to take it back. ''Not just that you're Devlin O'Hara, but of the man who made the name his.''

''Long story.'' Now the grin was rueful.

''We have the rest of the day with no telephone or chores requiring electricity to intrude.'' In a voice that was gentle and pensive, she added, ''If need be, we have the night.''

''No music?''

His smile altered again, but she wanted the blue fire, the mischief, the joy. ''This is your day, and your night, not mine.''

Devlin still had no idea where to start, or what to say, so he began with his family. "There are five of us. Three boys and two girls, the luckiest children in the world. Lucky in our parents, and in each other. All so much alike, yet each uniquely different. We were close as children and even closer as adults. Not often in proximity, but always in our hearts."

Kate watched his expression mellow and the lines in his forehead ease as he reminisced. She wondered if he could guess he was describing the family she'd always wanted.

"When Patience was six and I twelve, with the others falling between, to make sure we would always be close, we cut our palms and mingled our blood to make the bond stronger."

"Brothers and sisters by birth. Comrades by the rite of blood." Unconsciously stroking the ridged scar across his palm, in her mind Kate could picture five little O'Haras, wiry bodies tanned by the sun, huddled together. With Devlin the tallest, the darkest, the most handsome, leading their vow of fealty forever. She didn't know he was tallest, or that he was their leader and the most handsome, but she would stake heart and soul on it. "Comrades forever, with the scars as proof."

Devlin's hand closed convulsively over hers. "Regrettably, no." Beyond the denial he offered no explanation, for there was more to tell before then. "Like you, we traveled. Our parents took us everywhere, taught us everything. Or so it seemed. As we grew older, we went separate ways. Patience, into veterinary medicine. Tynan, eventually, to Montana. Valentina and Kieran, by one route or another to The Black Watch. And I? I was the oldest, the one in whom the wanderlust was strongest.

"Until I found Denali. Then, for the first time, I'd found a home. A place I wanted to stay. A place for roots."

Kate had never had a home. Not of the lasting sort.

She'd longed for that special place, for the traditions, the favorite things, the stability. Quietly, as if by raising her voice she might break the spell of his narration, she asked, "What was it that drew you to Denali?"

Devlin looked down at their joined hands, resting on his thigh. With the pad of his thumb stroking the translucent flesh of her knuckles, he answered as honestly as he knew how. "At first it was the excitement of the mountain, the sheer wonder of the challenge. Flying over the ice, landing on glaciers. But in the long run, it was as much the friends I found there." Shaking his head he rephrased. "No. Most of all it was the friends I found."

Kate was fascinated by his story, and with the man she saw as he spoke of his brothers, his sisters, and the days before the smile left his eyes. It wasn't plausible to believe his life had been perfect until then, but to Kate it was more than she'd ever dared to dream.

Or so she thought until he drew a long, shuddering breath and spoke again. "I didn't know what I was searching for, or even that I was searching, until I found Denali. In that unexpected corner of the world I had everything." His stroking finger moved over her hand, once, twice, then was still. Lifting his head, he fixed his riveting gaze on Kate. And in it she saw the hurt and pain she'd suspected magnified tenfold. The beautiful blue gaze was dulled, glazed. The eyes that looked to her and then through her were the eyes of a stranger.

"I had everything I ever wanted, and more," he said again, softly, his voice hoarse with grief and guilt. Looking away, he stared into a distant void, as if he couldn't bear to see her, to let her see him. Or to continue.

Her anger long dissipated, Kate waited, lost, puzzled, even afraid, with her hand still resting beneath his.

Slowly, inch by dreaded inch, his gaze returned to her, focusing on hers. "For that little while the world was a perfect place," he said bleakly. "Until I killed Joy Bohannon."

Six

Kate sat in a daze. As the color drained from her face, she looked away from wondrously beautiful eyes that looked as if they had beheld the end of his own world. Slowly, as if drawn by a will greater than her own, beneath lowered lashes Kate stared down at her hand in his. Devlin's dark, broad, scarred, gentle hand.

...killed Joy Bohannon.

...killed.

...killed.

The broken words echoed again and again in her mind, reverberating like a damning chant in her heart.

"No." Her denial was a hoarse whisper born on a rasping breath she didn't know she'd caught and held. Catching another, she turned her head a bare fraction. With her hair swinging heavily against her cheek, shielding her stunned dismay only a little, she repeated her answer in unwavering disbelief, "Never."

He'd come to the island a stranger. An intriguing, disarming intruder she'd wanted away and gone. Away from the island. Gone from her life. He'd stayed instead, becoming a familiar part of this place she'd come to regard as home. Then, as quickly, as inexplicably, he was firmly entrenched in her thoughts, and increasingly an integral part of her life.

Even as she wished him away, she'd been drawn to him. She'd set limits, he'd kept to them. She turned him away, he went, but not very far. She stumbled, and he was there, offering only kindness and strength. And only when she would accept them.

No matter who had sent him, or why he'd come, in her unflinching honesty, Kate could not help but admit Devlin had made her world a better place.

"No, Devlin," she whispered again, as if saying the word enough would make the memory of his confession go away. With her fingers still laced through his, keeping her gaze on their joined hands, she avowed with regained composure, "I might be uncertain of your reason for coming to Belle Terre, I might question who sent you and why. I might resent the need or the choice. I might have wished you away from the island and out of my life. But don't ask me to believe you would deliberately hurt anyone. Least of all, a woman. I won't even think it. I can't."

"Hey." Brushing away the curtain of her hair, letting his fingertips linger at her temple as he tucked the gold strand behind her ear, he smiled a dry nonsmile. "Who are you trying to convince? Yourself, darlin', or me?"

Nonplussed and oddly distracted for a moment, Kate kept her head bowed, reflecting on how much their joined hands were like them. Different in so many ways, and yet so much alike. Devlin's hands were bigger, darker, stronger. The truly masculine, truly capable hands of an adventurer. Hands roughened by his labors and marked by the scars that mapped his past. Her own hands were strong and, in their given right, capable. The secret tools of her trade. Weapons of mayhem, and even death, if need be.

Simon had seen to that.

Yet they were utterly feminine hands, smooth and slender. To the unaware they were no more than the hands of an accomplished pianist, a fastidious model, a boardroom peacemaker. And fragile in contrast to the inherent masculinity of Devlin's.

One could be perceived as harsh, even brutal, master of powerful deeds. The other as frail, defenseless, inured in decorum and grace. Neither was true. Just as she knew it wasn't true that Devlin had taken a life.

Breaking away from her musing she lifted her head and her gaze to Devlin's. "I'm not trying to convince anyone of anything. Nor can you, or any who might try, make me believe you killed someone. Not Joy Bohannon." The clasp of her hand was harsh, her nails driving home the strength of her conviction. "Not anyone."

Devlin had watched her silently, waiting for the revulsion and the horror that would send him away. He'd almost wished for it. Hoping he wouldn't have to tell her the whole of it. For then he must watch her face again, perhaps seeing worse than revulsion and horror as she understood how, for an act of monstrous and criminally arrogant misjudgment, more than a life was lost.

"God help me, Kate," he said at last, his face and voice somber. "I wish I deserved such trust. But I don't." Slipping his hand from her grasp, he left the sofa to stalk to the windows. The water was calming, but it would be hours, maybe days, before the serene sea of the peaceful low country returned. He wondered if he would be here to see that serenity, or that peace. "Dear heaven! You can't know how much I wish I could go back, undo it all."

Turning, one hand in his jeans' pocket, the other a tight,

impotent fist, he faced her, ready to tell the truth that would
damn him. "I took a dream from a woman, and the
greatest love of his life from my best friend. Neither can
ever be undone."

Once, on the day he brought coffee and stayed for the
breakfast he prepared, Kate had wondered if there was a
woman in his life. She'd thought not, then. She couldn't
explain her reaction, but she had been certain. Moments
ago, when he'd called Joy Bohannon's name with such
despair, for one immeasurable instant that surety was
shaken. But only for that instant. Listening now, one could
rush into sordid conclusions of an illicit affair. Of love
gone wrong, and wife-stealing friends. But these occurred
to Kate only for dismissal. Neither more than chaff to be
disposed of, in order to see and understand the truth.

Kate played hunches and obeyed instincts in her work
as mediator. Hunches and instincts had kept her one step
beyond the head games the cunning of the world were
wont to play.

But when she left the sofa to go to Devlin, she was
spurred by more than the instinct and intuition of a professional. The most basic factors that had drawn her to
him in the beginning drew her to him now. The simple
faith of a woman, and her trust in a special man.

With her fingers circling his wrist above the clenched
fist, she looked up into the bleak, grieving face. In calm
and quiet words barely audible above the pounding surf,
she asked, "Will you tell me about Joy?"

When it seemed as if he would never answer, with a
grim quirk of his lips, he nodded his stark assent.

As if it were her signal, yet in a move that seemed
totally unplanned and without premeditation, Kate stepped
closer. Releasing his wrist, she slipped her arms around
his waist, holding him as if she would console him.

Devlin was reeling, his mind chaotic. In a day he'd run

the gamut from friend to unwanted meddler and even traitor. From confessed killer, to this. He didn't know what her embrace meant. Kindness? Pity? Remorse? But did it matter?

Did anything matter, but that she looked like an angel? Or that her beguiling scent mingling with the rain was intoxicating? Did any of anything matter when the touch of her body, and the heat of it reaching out to warm him and comfort him, was the gentle trust he'd never hoped would be his?

He'd offered her his strength, and even in a seething dilemma she'd almost yielded. Almost, until a renewed surge of anger at his deceit turned him away. Now, as he'd offered her the ugly truth in one of the worst moments of his life, she'd come to him, forgetting her anger, refusing to believe, offering her tender strength for him to take.

And he felt so damnably, wonderfully good with her arms around him, with her golden eyes looking up at him with marvelous, restored trust. So good, he could almost believe that in her eyes he could be the man he'd been. The man who loved life and lived the gift of every minute to the fullest. The man before Denali.

Could he be that man again? With Kate to hold and to keep? And with her trust? Could it be? His desperate thought was a prayer, a dream, a mournful wish.

But it was too soon, there was more to tell. More ugliness. More horror. Taking her by the shoulders, his fingers flexing against the need to draw her closer, steeling himself against the need to take one kiss, he moved her from him.

"You said there was a story here. There is," he murmured quietly into the aura of her scent that seemed to enfold him even as the space widened between them. "You said you should hear it." The rasp of his words rattled in the still air, lingering in his mind like a toll for the lost. Letting his hands fall from her at last, he said what he must. "You should."

Kate searched his face. The sadness was there in his eyes tenfold. Whoever Joy Bohannon was, whatever happened on Denali, when she died, so did the smile in his eyes. So did a wonderful part of Devlin O'Hara, the man who loved women.

He didn't want to relive that awful time, but he would, for her sake. And oddly, it was for his sake that she would listen.

Linking her fingers through his again, she smiled up at him. Her heart hurt at the broken, faltering effort he tried in return.

"Come with me, Devlin." The word was an invitation and a plea. As she moved toward the sofa, it took only a little tug for him to follow. Once there, with a hand on his shoulder, Kate guided him to his seat, yet didn't take her own. Instead she crossed to a small, exquisitely stocked bar, studying shelves and new and aged bottles for a thoughtful moment, before choosing a wine.

Devlin watched each careful, efficient move as she dispensed with ceremony and expertly drew the cork. Paying even less homage to the pretenses often accompanying the partaking of the finer vintages, she splashed a few ounces in one gracefully unadorned glass, and then another.

Even in the increasing gloom, the wine swaying within the fluted crystal sparkled and shimmered like a living ruby. A stunning sight, but never as stunning as the woman who came to him.

He wanted her so badly he ached in every inch of his body. She was in his blood, in his mind and heart, in his thoughts. She was the center of his life and his desire as no woman had ever been.

Of course there had been women in the life of a man like Devlin O'Hara. Some whose faces and names he didn't remember. Some he would never forget. Some, passing acquaintances whose lives touched his in some way that led to lust or mutual hunger. Some, friends who shared a need and a moment.

But none had ever been lovers. Not in the sense of what the name meant to Devlin.

He had loved them, the women he forgot and the women he remembered. But to be lovers, lust or hunger or need weren't enough. Being in love, the forever kind shared by true lovers, had never touched him. Until now. Until Kate.

Until it was too late.

As he took the glass, his fingers closed over hers, briefly allowing one secret, yearning touch. "Thank you, Kate."

"For the wine?" Kate didn't know what prompted her question. Maybe it was the tone of his words, maybe the expression on his face. Maybe it was the way he spoke her name. Or only intuition, the impression there was more.

Devlin's only response was a slight tilt of his lips as he considered her question. Yes, for the wine, but for so much more. For the days on the island, for the walks, for whales and turtles. For her childish delight in angel wings, the delicate shell she loved best of all.

And even for this day.

Not just for this day, he amended in his mind. *Especially* for this day. For believing, for a little while.

Smiling his half smile, he lifted his glass in a small salute to the woman who would never know that he'd fallen a little in love with her in a crowded grocery. Then completely, as he sat on a lonely, moonlit beach listening to night music. And now, irrevocably, as she watched him over a glass of wine, with faith brimming in her eyes.

"For that first day in Ravenel's, for music on the beach," he said at last, with an honesty she would never know. Then sobering, he murmured, "Most of all, for the wine."

Kate was puzzled, but said nothing as he drew her down to the sofa. Setting her barely tasted wine aside, she folded her hands in her lap and listened to a story of happenstance, impossible courage, and life and death.

"I don't imagine it comes as any surprise to you that I've worked at a lot of jobs in a lot of places, and played twice as hard in many more." His lips quirked, more in a grimace than a disparaging smile. "For me, it was always the challenges in life that mattered. Before one was done, I was looking for the next. Constantly ready to move on. Until Denali."

Denali. He said the name with such a mix of emotions, Kate almost reached out to comfort him. But this was his story, ghastly or wonderful, he must tell it as he wished, without distraction. Or even solace.

"She offered everything I ever wanted, all I'd spent half my life searching for. Each day was that wonderful challenge, a never-ending adventure. And when the day was done, there were the people. People like me, like Jock Bohannon, and Joy."

She. Denali. It didn't surprise Kate that he called the mountain she. He might hate it now, but once he loved it. As he loved all women, with honor and reverence. Daring a single comment that seemed relevant, she said, quietly, "You loved her."

"I loved them both. They were special people apart, and even more special together. Every man and woman in Talkeetna admired and wished for what they saw in Jock and Joy."

Kate had spoken of the mountain, not Joy Bohannon, but she didn't correct him. For she understood. Her parents were like that. Wonderful in their own right. Spectacular and unique, a couple complete, as they lived and died together.

"Every now and then a love like Jock and Joy's comes

along, making those around them happier and better. Until
I met them, I never knew there was an emptiness in my
life. I never thought I could settle in one place. When I
did, I was a while realizing that love like theirs only comes
along once in a thousand lifetimes, and the rest of the
world must stand in its reflection looking on. But for the
little time I knew them, even that was enough.

"Then I made a mistake and a terrible error in judgment.
I played a hunch that went wrong, and Joy died."

With the last, Devlin fell silent. He seemed to retreat
from her, perhaps with his thoughts taking him back to
Denali. Kate finished what he couldn't. "Your plane went
down on the summit."

"Yes." The single word was flat, lifeless.

"Jock wasn't with you?"

Lifting his head, he stared out the windows at the shore
and the sea, but it was sharp, snow-covered peaks he saw.
"Until the day of the crash, Joy never went to the slopes.
Jock led the expeditions, she seemed content to stay home.
No one knew why, that's just the way it was. Even so, I
didn't question when she came to me asking that I fly her
to base camp, to meet Jock. She was happy, almost giddy.

"Joy was always happy, but I'd never seen her quite
like she was that day. So eager, so full of life. Bursting
with an inner joy." Turning to Kate, as if he'd forgotten,
then remembered she was there, he asked, "Did I tell you
Jock called her his joyful girl?"

Kate's answer to his poignant question was low, hoarse
with heartache. "No, Devlin, you didn't tell me."

"He did, for that's what she was, joyful."

Devlin was delaying the worst. Gently, Kate prompted.
"Joy wanted to go to base camp to meet Jock. And you
agreed?"

"We never made it. A storm came up, veering from one
side of the mountain to the other. A freak, the worst kind.

I didn't think we could make it through to the camp, and we couldn't turn back. That's when I opted to go around. That was my gamble, the wrong call. When we went down, crashing, burning, we weren't where we were expected to be. Then the storm veered back, catching us in the middle, without shelter, and with little hope of being found.''

Kate knew then that the scars on his palms had come from the burning plane. How valiantly he must have fought it. How strong he must have been, for Joy.

"I made a judgment call," Devlin repeated. "I was wrong. Because of it, the search and rescue teams were days finding us. Days, and an hour too late. She died there in the snow. Joy and her dreams of carrying a baby beneath her heart. A baby she and Jock had never thought they might have. Never dared to even imagine having."

"She was going to tell him an impossible dream might come true," Kate ventured, as her heart broke anew for this gallant man.

"Only Jock knew she'd had a serious case of rheumatic fever as a child. And even he didn't know she'd been seeing a doctor, who monitored her carefully and had finally given his okay for a baby. At last Joy could give her beloved Jock something she'd always wanted for him. Instead, I took Joy from him."

Kate wanted to argue, but he was too adamant to believe, and too worn down by the telling to listen. All she could offer was a comforting touch, and, if he were a different man, a shoulder to lean on. But this was Devlin, the gallant. Taking his hands in hers she stroked the scars she was certain were the badge of a living grief. Just as certainly, she knew that no one but he would know or understand completely the horror of the mountain.

Throughout the whole story Devlin had relived the hours and the days, looking inward, never at Kate. Now he turned to her, his face ashen, his eyes dark and brooding as he searched her face. Catching the glint of tears in her eyes, he touched her cheek, cradling it in his palm, brushing the dampness away with a caress. "For Joy?"

"For Joy, for her hope for a baby." Catching his hand, keeping it at her cheek, she said truthfully, "Most of all for you."

"For me?"

"For a good man caught in an impossible situation. Giving his best against greater and more impossible odds. A man who selflessly waged a terrible battle few would fight, and only a miracle could win."

"If that were only true." His words were ragged with despair of failure. "If I'd had the sense not to take Joy to altitudes her damaged heart couldn't stand. Then maybe the cold wouldn't have…"

"Is another of your sins that you aren't a mind reader?" Kate interrupted, stemming the flow. "Were you supposed to divine what Joy Bohannon had told no one in all of Talkeetna?"

"I should have…"

"You should have… what?" Kate's eyes were blazing now as she dragged his hand from her cheek, but kept it in her grasp. "Refused a friend, saying, 'No, I won't take you to base camp because there's a freak storm brewing and our plane will go down, and your damaged heart won't stand the cold?'"

"Don't make fun." Devlin's hand turned in hers, his grasp hard and punishing.

Kate was as unaware of the powerful grip as Devlin. "I'm not making fun, I'm making a point. A truth."

"You don't know, you weren't there."

"I know you, that's enough." Only a short time ago she'd accused him of subterfuge, now she realized that deep in her mind and heart, she'd never believed it of him.

"I know how much you care, especially when women are concerned."

"You're assuming, Kate."

"I've seen it. Today for Tessa, when a sixth sense compelled you to brave a storm. For what?" There was passion in her voice. A passion absent for far too long. "For a little girl you don't know. Why? Because you thought she might need someone. On a lesser note, there was Officer O'Brian. You made her smile. You made her happy. For a reason, yes, but also for herself. Because you care, Devlin. For Tessa, for Officer O'Brian. And for Joy Bohannon."

Hearing her own words ringing with fervor through the gathering gloom of the room, Kate knew then why his sister had sent her brother to Summer Island. They were the perfect match for Valentina's purpose. Kate Gallagher was a troubled woman, and Devlin O'Hara was a man who needed to care again.

"I can only tell you what I believe, Devlin." He was a man who hid behind his laughter, but the fatigue wouldn't be hidden. Kate wondered if he'd truly slept in weeks, even months.

Because he was too quiet, and so obviously consumed by his own thoughts, and because she couldn't sit there watching the hurt and grief that marked his face, Kate stood, taking up his empty glass. As she crossed the room to pour more from the aged bottle, she felt his gaze follow. But when her own was irresistibly drawn to him again, she couldn't begin to interpret the change she saw in him. The fatigue was still starkly visible, but there was something more. Something she'd never seen in Devlin.

Puzzled, Kate looked away and, turning a little clumsy under his intense scrutiny, spilled a bit of the wine. The dark vermilion splashed in droplets across the creamy skin of her wrist like a string of delicate rubies. Without think-

ing, she brought her arm to her lips and with her tongue
swept the wine away.

Devlin made a sound. She thought he'd spoken and she
hadn't heard. But when she let her eyes lift again to meet
his look, nothing had changed. He hadn't moved, the mark
of his pallor hadn't calmed, and the intensity with which
he watched her hadn't eased.

Crossing back to him, she set the bottle on the table by
his side, then offered the refilled glass. As he took it from
her, she turned away, but his fingers circling her wrist drew
her back.

"Play for me, Kate."

It didn't occur to her to refuse. Refusing wouldn't have
been an option she could choose. "What would you like
me to play?"

"Anything."

The pad of his fingers lay lightly on the throbbing veins
of her wrist. Kate wondered if he could feel the leap in
her pulse beneath his compelling touch. "I'll play for you,
Devlin," she said in a voice barely above a whisper. "For
as long as you like."

With a small sound, he leaned back, losing himself in
the glittering depths of his glass. Yet, when she began to
play, he looked up, finding her limned by reflections from
the sea and shore. As if it were for his pleasure alone, the
light danced across her lovely features, blazed like flame
through the gold and silver of her tumbled hair, then sifted
down her body to mold the lines of her breasts and waist
in degrees of shadow.

Watching her move, mesmerized by the flow of her
hands across the keys and calmed by the most subdued
and tranquil music he'd ever heard her play, proved the
perfect seduction for a stubborn and tormented mind. Sipping the wine she'd chosen so carefully, letting the smooth,
ripe flavor lie on his tongue like old, sweet memories, he

felt the tension in the powerful muscles of his body begin to ease. And as she wrapped him in her quiet, peaceful music, afternoon slipped unnoticed into evening.

Shadows spilled from distant corners of the room, creeping with little haste across the floor like the rise of a lazy tide. Devlin's lashes dipped to his cheeks, shutting out the vision of Kate, and then her music. The glass tumbled from his fingers, the crystal sounding the note of a distant chime.

Kate faltered at the tiny knell, but with no more than an ebb in the sweeping melody, she played on. For an hour past the time he fell asleep, she continued to play. Mozart, Beethoven, DeBussy, Bach, Chopin, even venturing into the gentler modern composers.

When the darkness was complete, with only a sliver of moon lighting the sky, her fingers drifted one last time over the chords of her favorite sonata and withdrew to her lap. For a time she sat, not moving, hoping he wouldn't wake. Finally, with only the sound of the restless tide lapping at dunes for music, and the fingernail moon for light, she left the piano. Crossing to him, she knelt at his feet, retrieving the glass that had proven sturdier than its delicate stem and bowl would appear.

Rising again, intending to leave the sleeping man in peace, she found that she couldn't look away from him. In concert the pale darkness and the cloak of sleep had wiped the mark of tragedy from his face, leaving it the unmarred countenance of a provocative and attractive man. When she'd first seen him in Ravenel's on a day that seemed a lifetime ago, his hair was longer than she liked. In his days on the island he hadn't bothered finding a barber, resorting instead to the colorful bandannas to control the wave that tended to fall over his forehead.

He'd worn the cattleman's hat in the rain, and there was no bandanna. Without its restraint, gleaming blacker than black in the dim reflection of moonlight filtering through the windows, the lock brushed the level sweep of his brows.

As she'd played she'd dreamed of sweeping back the lock, of letting it slip though her fingers like coarse silk, of feeling the crisp wealth of it against her palm. Now, with a need that was overwhelming, she wanted to touch him. She wanted him to open his eyes, to look at her without the blinding haze of pain. She wanted to find tenderness in his gaze.

More than anything she wanted the wicked, teasing grin that was irresistible. With it she wanted laughter that would set the blue fire ablaze in his eyes forever.

Deep in her soul, she knew she wanted Devlin himself. Sad or wickedly teasing, with blue fire or only embers, she wanted him.

Kate Gallagher, who through the years had never understood the mystery of the sexual attractions and alliances of her peers and colleagues, knew at last what it was to need a man. To hunger for a man's caress, for his kiss. For all that he was, or would be.

She didn't intend to follow the dream, but before she realized, her fingers glided into his luxurious hair, brushing it away from a barely lined forehead. Until the innocence of true sleep, she hadn't realized how strongly the burden of his recent past affected his appearance. In this rare moment she saw the daring drifter who loved life and lived it to the fullest. The gentle knight who would have tempted and loved the women who crossed his path. Young or old, how wonderfully he would have loved them.

"And bless you, Devlin O'Hara," she murmured. "How the fortunate must have loved you."

In a move as swiftly violent as a flash of lightning, a hand clamped around her wrist like a vise, dragging her down.

Stifling a cry as the rescued wineglass fell on the sofa

and away from harm, she said with quiet calm, "It's Kate, Devlin. You're here with me, safe on Summer Island."

A strong arm continued to bear her down. A half-muttered cry sounded in her ear as his hot breath grazed her cheek. As another hand burrowed beneath her hair, cradling and shielding her face against his chest, she understood the desperate and guttural word rumbling in its depths.

Fire.

With her peaceful music lulling him into vulnerable oblivion, the Denali of his unguarded nights had come for him. But the monolith wouldn't destroy this day or this night with its horror and grief, Kate vowed. Not because of her, or her music.

"Devlin." Wrapping her hand around his as he clamped harder over her wrist, she murmured at last, "Please."

The softly spoken word swept away the torpor of sleep. Though his eyes were half open he hadn't seen beyond his dream. Now a gaze as intense as midnight focused on her shadowed face. "Kate."

"Yes," she murmured in tender assurance. Slipping free of his loosening clasp, she stroked his face.

"I hurt you…"

"Never." Touching his lips, she stopped his stumbling words. The contact was like magic trembling between them. Magic drawing her yearning mouth down to his kiss.

"Kate." He called her name again in quiet reverence. And as his arms closed around her, with Denali and the past forgotten, she heard him whisper, "My love."

Seven

My love.

As the last tarrying dregs of sleep vanished, with his own words ringing in his mind and his heart, Devlin fiercely caught her to him. As he lowered her to the sofa, his body sprawled hard and intimately against her. Yet lying lean hip against narrow shapely hip with one burly thigh pinioning long legs that never seemed to end was not nearly close enough.

Sliding the length of her, molding the solid planes of his body against yielding curves, he rose over her. With his arms framing her face, his blue gaze shadowed and unreadable, he stared down into golden eyes. Slowly his expression altered from one of near anguish to a questioning exploration.

For what seemed an eternity, his look searched deeply within hers, as if he would see into her heart, her soul. Sighing raggedly at what he read in her face even in dusky light, his head dipped slowly, purposely, his lips brushed hers. Once, twice, meeting her welcoming surrender, and he was lost.

With the fleeting touch of that perfect mouth, something beyond taming was set free. In the wake of heartache allayed, the bittersweet longings of weeks reconciled into one boundless need.

Tenderness flying in the face of his yearning, his mouth ground in demand against hers. His plundering tongue was seeking and ardent. Holding Kate, kissing her, taking the sweetness of her mouth, was manna for a starving man. A feast for the ravenous. But there could be no ease with only a kiss.

Not now. Not ever. The indomitable passion would not be conquered, nor the primal hunger sated by less than all she was. Now that desires, couched so long in remorse, had been set free, no restraint would quell them. There could be no calming peace or ease for Devlin, but Kate, her body, and her love.

There was no help for it. No help for either of them. Wherever this night led, whatever the consequence of this moment, there was no other path.

One unsteady hand tangling in her hair, the other supporting him, Devlin lifted his head, leaving her mouth moist and beloved. As he looked down in reverence and barely leashed greed, the heat of their bodies fusing into a heady mix of his scent and hers drew him back again. To her lips, to her body, without a will of his own, like a lodestone.

But this time his kiss was grazing, transient. Ever adoring. The touch of his tongue as he traced the pout of her lower lip, light and fleeting. A provocative promise of a man, whispering of abiding, smoldering need.

Provocative promises. The wicked, enticing allusion of undiscovered delight. And, for Devlin, a covenant of love.

Twice more he kissed her. A man drinking deeply, then deeper from a well of wonder. Each time he withdrew, each time he returned. Each time he teased and caressed, with his lips, with his tongue, with the burgeoning virility of his lean and powerful body.

Kate met his kiss with a kiss, his caress with a caress. With each unspoken promise she made one of her own as she opened to Devlin like a morning glory to the sun.

His touch drew her further into madness. Retreat left her bereft and lonely. Her mind was in total disarray, with no clear thought to serve as anchor. She was fearful though she knew there was nothing to fear. She was fretful and the reason eluded her. For the first time in her life there were needs beyond her control. A lusting hunger only Devlin could fulfill.

His body was hard and harsh in his own need as he leaned over her again to steal another kiss. To pillage lightly and quickly from her willing, parting lips. When he would have moved away to tease and cherish once more, with a strangled cry Kate clasped the nape of his neck, her fingers threaded through his hair. Her hoarsely urgent protest echoed within him, touching every sentient part of him. In that plaintive cry he heard passion as wild and hunger as primitive as his.

As she guided his mouth to hers, to claim kisses of her own, Devlin's fate was sealed for this moment and this day. But more than that, he knew it would be forever.

"No." The word was restraint, never denial, and his whisper was breathless and hoarse as he struggled away. Putting the little space he could bear between them, he contented himself with fingertips lying against the satin flesh of her nape, and the stroke of the pad of his thumb over the line of her jaw. "We can't, Kate," he muttered again, his tone a little unbelieving even as he reasoned with himself as well as with her. "Not like this."

Kate was bemused, her mind governed by her body and the tumult he'd fueled and ignited. All she grasped or could think was that he had gone too far from her. The separation was too empty and desolate without him.

When she reached out for him, his hand closed over hers, drawing her palm to his lips. Stroking her trembling flesh, his breath adding to the heat that threatened to consume her, he whispered, "No, sweetheart. No."

Kate made a small protesting sound. A lament of entreaty that made his heart soar.

"Shh, darlin'. Hush now," he whispered into the hollow of her palm. "I'm going to make love to you. For as long as you want me and with all that I am, I'm going to love you. But not here."

As he stroked away the moisture left by his kiss, Kate shivered and her fingers convulsed over his. Devlin turned his head slowly in a small and solemn denial of surging passion. Mustering every share of O'Hara fortitude and honor, determined, he stood fast. "Not like this. No quick, awkward tumble on a stranger's sofa with our clothes torn away in haste and the heat of passion."

Breaking off, he chuckled hoarsely, but with little humor, at the vision of Kate in nothing but a shirt opened a challenging inch or two. "On second thought—" lashes dipped over a steady blue gaze "—maybe someday." Brows slanted wickedly, blue eyes traced the line of her throat to the shadowed cleft of her breasts, and for a brief instant he was the teasing Devlin of old as he amended, "Most assuredly, I promise, someday."

Then, as quickly as it had come, the small humor vanished. "But, my dear love," he murmured softly, "never our first time."

Standing in an unhurried move, then folding his hand more securely over hers, he brought her up with him. When she swayed, her body leaning into his, he was there to hold her. But the touch of his body was more than support, more than substance and strength. He was power and valor, honor and temptation incarnate. With every rugged plane, every muscle and sinew a caressing flame reminding her of the inferno that threatened.

Clinging to him as she'd never clung to anyone, she repeated in words that were both question and affirmation, "Our first time."

"Yes," he answered in hushed assurance. "The first and the perfect time for all the other times to follow." With a finger at her chin, he raised her fathomless gaze to his. "You must know this is more than sex, more than a fling answering the heat of lust. I've had my share of one-night stands in the past. But this isn't the past, and I promise you, once will never be enough for either of us."

Bending to her, raking his fingers through her hair and framing her face with the heels of his hands, he let his probing look range over her. From the top of her head to the fullness of her breasts, his look touched and searched and lingered, returning, at last, to recapture her gaze with his. Holding her spellbound with a look and a gentle clasp, he questioned softly, "You understand, don't you, that this is only the beginning?"

Kate's lashes fluttered down, but only to ease a moment of turmoil before capturing and keeping the glittering stare of sapphire eyes turned to midnight. Because what she saw in that glitter raged within her, as well, she was not shocked by the bold, bottomless desire. Nor by his promise of a time to come.

No. The silent reprise rang in her fevered thoughts. As surely as his touch was kindness and madness in one, as surely as she'd given herself up to the primal male and his primal needs, as surely as she would again, there must be more.

Shivering at the magnitude of his promise, Kate's lashes

brushed her cheeks, shielding her eyes. For one short moment she wanted to step back, to move away from Devlin
and the wild, sweet magic he wove. For one short moment
she wanted to cling to the past, to hide in the safety and
penance of grief and guilt. In a perverse way it was fright-
ening to forsake emotions that had been her constant companions, perhaps her asylum, for months. She was tempted
to hold them like a bulwark before her, but she couldn't.

Even knowing that in the return of saner times, grief
and guilt would increase tenfold, a hundredfold, she
couldn't.

In deliberate decision, her lashes lifted. The eyes that
looked out at Devlin from the shelter of the gold-tipped
fringe were the unfaltering regard of a tigress. Her face
was a study in contrast marked by light and darkness, and
so lovely she set his heart hammering in his chest, and the
blood coursing through his body at a demented speed.

Devlin, the fearless, who had faced true tigers on the
plains of India, and in the jungles of Africa, felt his knees
give with the weight of waiting for her response.

Her meticulous study roamed his face as she raised her
hand to curl her palm about his cheek. Letting it slide ever
so slowly to his jaw, her eyes followed, their solemn regard settling on his lips in arrant fascination as one finger
traced their line from corner to corner. Not taking her finger away, she paused at one sensitive corner that quirked
as a muscle in his jaw tensed.

Drawing a long, hesitant breath, at last she admitted with
unexpected candor, "I know."

Devlin wasn't certain he heard her correctly. And, for a
dreading instant, the old doubts came flooding back. But
only for an instant, no more. There was too much between
them, what he felt and what he recognized in Kate was
too strong for doubt.

Turning his head only the little needed to touch his lips

to hers, he reveled in her strength, and her desire. A guttural groan rumbling in his throat, he tore himself from her kiss, and sweeping her into his arms, stalked the interminable length of the narrow hall leading to her bedroom.

Steam rose around her, warm and soothing. Muscles she hadn't realized were tense relaxed. The shower was a luxury she hadn't anticipated. Even with no electricity for most of the day, she hadn't thought to start the generator. But Devlin had assured her it would take more than part of a day to cool the tank.

With that assurance, he'd virtually herded her into the bath, urging that she take her time. Confused and, yes, she would admit it, a little wounded by his poised demeanor, she'd done as he asked. Now, she stood beneath the pelting shower hoping to wash away the unresolved torment smoldering only hotter within her.

Perhaps the muscles had begun to relax with the steam and heat, but a part of her mind, only newly wakened, had not. Not by one part, parcel, or fragment, it hadn't.

Closing the taps at last, she stood with her hands braced on the tile wall, her thoughts scurrying, wondering what she would find when she walked through the door. What waited for her in the darkness of this great house by the sea?

Would Devlin O'Hara be waiting for her? Would he be gone? From her bedroom, from the specter of her bed? From her life.

"He won't be." Her words echoed in the tile and glass enclosure of the shower. As she reached for a towel and, finally, her nightshirt, Kate knew Devlin waited.

The bedroom was not dark as Kate expected. Instead there were burning candles by the bed and scattered in

corners. In their wavering light the room took on a be-
witching ambience. The turned-down bed with its taupe
linens loomed prominently and shone like raw gold.
Across one pillow lay a rose from the climbing vine that
covered one wall by the pool. As her seasons on the island
had crept from summer into autumn, and the ancient vine
recovered from summer's unrelenting heat and humidity,
the blooms were profuse, the fragrance enchanting.

But a hundred blooms would never be as enchanting as
this single rose. There would never be another as breath-
taking as this gift of a tender lover. As its perfume mingled
with the scent of candles and a salt-laden breeze drifting
through open doors, Kate knew there would never be another as beguiling.

Candles to ease her way in the dark. A rose for her
pleasure. A turned-down bed to tempt. But no Devlin.

Yet Kate knew the wait for her lover would not be long.

Her sense of time suspended, taking the blossom from
the pillow, she brought it to her cheek, caressing her skin
with its soft petals, surrounding herself in its balm. As with
everything, the flowers of the island fascinated her. And
as with everything, she'd read and studied them, learning
that more than a century before, this delicate pink, with a
fragrance as delicate, had come by way of India in the
hold of a merchant ship.

In the renowned tradition of Southern reverence for
flowers and beauty, it was protected and reproduced, and
thus proliferated through the years. In those years it
adapted and flourished, until it grew, inherently, like a do-
mesticated wildflower.

Now with its petals shimmering as gossamer, and its
scent the incense of the night, it would linger forever in
her memory.

Returning the rose to the pillow, in a slow spin Kate
looked around her. Only a man of true passions, only a

romantic, would create such a mood. "Only a gentle dreamer," Kate whispered, as if with her voice she might shatter the enchantment he created. Smiling, she drew the backs of her fingers across the rose. "Devlin."

"Yes, my love?"

He stood in the doorway, the curtains billowing around him. Droplets of water clung to his hair and shoulders, and beaded his chest. Each brilliant sphere capturing the flame of candles in reflection. Beneath its sheen, his sun-burnished skin seemed darker still, in contrast to the im-maculate taupe towel draped about his hips and tucked securely at his waist. Kate knew then that while she show-ered, Devlin had gone to the sea.

Embers of desire banked only a little by the quiet time in the shower stirred at the sight of him. His body painted in dancing light and flickering shadows, with the last traces of the cleaving sea emulating fire, spoke of barely leashed carnal need, and the promise of an undiscovered paradise.

Kate's heart faltered at this sight of him...Devlin, as she'd never seen him. Brawny, vital, his eyes feverish and bright, his barely concealed body taut and on edge. The allusion of tensions, exhilaration, and pent-up energy seethed, as if an overpowering storm brewed within him, arousing him.

Shivering under the intensity of his fierce, searching study, and lifting her head a small challenging measure, she let her own stare contend with his, hotter and more scorching than any flame. Her cheeks paled, her eyes grew large, luminous, and in them there was desire for Devlin to see. For all the world to see.

But their world was here. Their world was now.

She had called his name, and he was there. But now he waited. Devlin, ever the gallant.

"I didn't want this..." Her voice broke and a tear glis-tened on her lashes.

Devlin watched and listened and endured with sincere concern and an iron control. Kate was proud and beautiful, and incredibly brave standing before him in pale candle-light. So proud and beautiful and brave he ached for her. The minute he stepped through the door, he saw she wore the familiar nightshirt. A wisp of orange silk flowing from her shoulders to the tips of her breasts, then falling away to scarcely skim her hips before ending a paltry inch above her knees.

She was naked beneath the shirt. Only a scrap of orange and four pearl buttons trailing from an unwitting décolletage halfway to the hem shielded from his sight what his heart and body wanted most desperately. In a strange way it seemed he had always wanted her most desperately. Even long before he knew her.

Soul mates, needing only the right time and place to come together? Had this moment been preordained? Devlin was the first son of an only son, not the seventh of the seventh, and he didn't know. In this time, he didn't care. All that mattered was another part of the equation that must be resolved before he could make her his.

Just one, he thought, gathering his strength as he heeded and attended the soft voice reaching out to him.

"I never meant this. After Paul, I was determined I would never want or need anyone." She turned to her bed where candles held the darkness at bay. In the spill of their light, the rose waited. Devlin's treasured rose.

"I told myself time and again that I wouldn't want you or need you for more than a friend. But from the moment you stood at my door with a cocky grin and a packet of pilfered coffee, I did. I have." She looked at him then. His teeth were clenched, rippling a muscle in his jaw. Framed by the shaggy disarray of his hair, tendons in his neck were starkly visible. His chest rose slowly in one carefully controlled breath after another.

She wanted to go to him, to offer an end to his anguish. But first there was more he should understand. More he should know. "Long ago, only months after I accepted Simon's invitation to become a part of The Black Watch, I vowed that if I couldn't love a man like Paul Bryce, I wouldn't love any man."

Devlin went very still. Nothing in the room seemed to move as even the breeze grew quiet. He felt as if the whole world held itself in abeyance in deference to the only issue that mattered. The truth of Kate Gallagher and Devlin O'Hara.

"I shouldn't want you. I shouldn't love you." With a tilt of her head, Kate glanced away, as if she were thinking and remembering. Slowly she turned again, her eyes rising to meet and keep his gaze unflinchingly. "But I do."

Her hands had been clasped tightly before her. Now her grip loosened and her arms dropped to her sides. Her fingers curled loosely in a posture that left her unguarded and vulnerable. But the wariness and uncertainty that had been in her voice were forgotten. And there was only tenderness and honesty in her face and her eyes. "I love you, Devlin O'Hara."

Devlin had little memory of going to her. In one second he stood in the doorway, in another she was in his arms. Her lips were on his, her hands clasped at his nape. A soft cry revealed her hunger, as wild and desperate and as great as his. As the towel loosened around his hips then slid to the floor, all he knew was that there was still a barrier between them.

Only the grip of his hands at her shoulders kept them from shaking as he moved her from him. "Shh, love," he whispered at her murmured objection. "Only a heartbeat, and this."

He wondered if his clumsy fingers could manage the four buttons, and when they slipped free, he was grateful

for silk and tiny pearls. Leaning forward, cupping her face
in his palms, he kissed her again, tracing the shape of her
mouth with his until her lips parted for him. He felt the
heat of her mouth meeting his and lost the sense of his
purpose.

It was only when she drew away to kiss his throat and
his chest that he felt the brush of her shirt against him and
remembered. Catching her wandering hands in his, he
drew them to his lips, leaving a kiss in each palm before
folding her fingers and releasing her.

"First, this," he whispered as he traced a line down
each side of her throat and over her shoulders, brushing
the shirt from her as he went. When the flame-colored silk
floated away to lie with the discarded towel, he sighed in
quiet relief. "And now, this."

Lifting her into this arms, he took her to the bed. Laying
her gently on taupe linen that had gleamed gold in little
light, he stared down at her, at Kate. His to cherish.

My love.

Devlin's own words rang in his mind and in his heart.
And he knew he meant them. All his life he'd called the
women he knew and cared for little pet names. Names that
ranged from teasing to comforting. But he'd never spoken
of love.

Love. A condition of the heart, and a word too serious
for platonic teasing.

The condition of his heart as she drew him down to her.
Down to her embrace and her kiss. To the storm of desire
that equaled his. Desire and passion reaching into the heart
of him, becoming a never-ending part of all he would ever
be.

As he turned with her, settling her over him to cradle
her body intimately with his, she went with him. Laughing
softly, exultantly, she rose over him, letting the sweep of
her hair and the exquisite scent of her entice and enfold

him. He reached for her. She caught his wrists, keeping them imprisoned by his own will. Setting her velvet trap, keeping him captive, for a long while, she looked down through candlelight. Down at their bodies contrasted in the dusk. Pale skin against dark, the strong and less strong, subtle femininity and aroused masculinity. Desire meeting desire.

When he would have spoken, she shook her head, then bent to his hostage kiss. With each move the fullness of her breasts glided over his chest. The soft swell seducing and tormenting with nipples growing ever darker, ever more voluptuous, with each contact.

Her first kiss had been fleeting, almost poignant. The pain and pleasure of it left him wanting more. Yet he was afraid that in his consuming need, he would move too fast, and want too much. When he lifted her over him, relinquishing control, he thought to calm the building fury. Now he realized the error of any thought or effort seeking to maintain control.

Twice more he suffered the whetting, enticing, punishment of her kiss and caress. And when he could stand no more, he drew her down and beneath him.

"My turn," he growled roughly, softly, gently.

This time it was Kate who would speak, and Devlin who stopped her words with a shake of his head and a kiss. This time it was she who was held in gentle restraint for the sweet torture of his lovemaking.

This time it was he who rose over her to trace the elegant line of her brows, to stroke the butterfly brush of her lashes, and the angle of her cheek. When a knuckle grazed lightly over the corner of her mouth, her indrawn breath was a slow, shuddering gasp.

Devlin heard and his body responded, but he neither paused nor altered the course of his delightful, meandering quest. The roughened but gentle fingertips stroked the line

of her jaw and the length of her throat. Then rested for a
moment at the throbbing, shadowed hollow at its base.

As he watched, her gaze dropped and her lashes fluttered
yet again. Her breathing grew slow and shallow, as if waiting. He hoped needing and wanting, as much as he.

Slowly, never taking his gaze from her shielded eyes,
he let his touch glide lazily from her throat. Halting
abruptly, his hand poised and ready, he heard the uneven
rhythm of her labored breaths, and saw the darkness of
eyes with pupils dilated until irises diminished to slender
bands of gold.

He thought she would speak her desire, revealing her
needs. But she kept silent, watching him, waiting for him.

Instead it was he who spoke, but with a suckling kiss
as he cupped her breasts and lifted the tight budding nipples to the reverent stroke and gentle pull of his lips.

With each touch, each stroke of his tongue, each intimate revelation, she sighed and wept. Clasping him closer,
she writhed against him, needing that she be a part of him,
and he of her.

When that moment came, when passion so carefully
guarded would not be contained, with bodies in concert,
they rode the storm together. Together, ever together, until
Kate's shuddering cry was joined by his.

This was the first and, as he promised, the perfect time.
The time for all to follow.

Long into the night he held her, watching her drowse
and wake, and drowse again. When a clock struck the hour
of a new day, she roused and turned to him. With petals
of the shattered rose filling the bed with their scent, he
made love to her.

And longer still into the night, at the chime of another
hour, again.

Sated and spent, and deliciously weary, as the flame of
the last candle guttered and died, Kate turned her face into

the hollow of his throat. With the taste of the sea on her lips and the weight of his hand at her breast, she whispered simply, "Devlin."

When she woke, he was gone.

Raising her head from the pillow, with her body supported by her bent arms, Kate looked around the room. Nothing had changed. Somehow, she thought it would. After the night with Devlin, she expected the whole world would have changed.

But the light of day still slanted through open doors. The sea still whispered in harmony with crying gulls. Palmettos stirred by a passing breeze still rustled against windows. If she looked out, the sky would still be blue. The beach would be silver sand. And Sea Watch still sat securely on massive beams.

As her look ranged over the room, she realized the candles had been taken away. No sea-swept towel lay on the floor where it had been dropped heedlessly. The orange nightshirt draped circumspectly over a chair. Nothing was as it had been in the last minute before Devlin had taken her in his arms.

Beyond a mild fatigue and a few tender, achy body parts, and the fact that she'd never slept so well or so long, there was no evidence the interlude ever happened.

Interlude.

Was that all it was?

Sitting up, Kate studied her reflection through luminous eyes. Her hair was in appalling disorder, a casualty of repeated masculine caresses. Her face seemed pale, but her cheeks were flushed with the light abrading of a day-old beard. And her lips...

Staring at the stranger in the mirror, Kate touched her swollen mouth, tracing the shape as he had traced it, feeling again the kisses. Some tender and some not. Remembering his sweet, gentle touch, the driving desperation of his passion. His whispered words breathed against her skin, saying so little, yet so much. The vow Devlin made time and again, but never voiced.

Why? And why not? Kate's questions echoed hollowly in her thoughts. But she knew there were no answers within these walls.

Throwing back the sheet Devlin had gallantly drawn over her bare body before he left her, Kate glimpsed rose petals. Pink rose petals. Catching up a shattered few in her hands, she drew them to her face. Breathing deeply of their fragrance and their memories, she relived a night too wonderful. Then she smiled, letting each fall again to the rumpled sheets like blushing snowflakes.

The sun would still rise, and it would set. The rushing tides of the sea would ebb. The wind would blow and be still. Birds would sing, than fall silent. The order of the world would go on.

In a single night, only she had changed. Only Kate Gallagher, in a scattering of petals from Devlin's rose.

Rising from the bed, she went to the bath. Pausing before the long mirror there, she inspected her body, finding it was as always. Even her eyes. But Devlin had touched her and made love to her. And, no matter what might come of a single night, she would never be the same. In mind, in body, in heart.

Especially her heart, Kate believed as she stepped into a shower warmed again, as she made ready for a new day, and Devlin.

Eight

The house was empty. Silence resounded through each room, bearing her down in loneliness that weighed heavily on her mind and heart.

Strange, Kate thought as she wandered the house. Being alone rarely bothered her. For, in her memories, she'd always been alone, standing on the outside of close-knit circles looking in.

She'd never doubted she was a much beloved child. Yet, with precocious perception, she'd always known the love her parents shared was so all-consuming she was the extra. Deeply cherished as the expression of their singular devotion, indulged and adored, but always with the constant awareness of being the outsider.

Modeling and the cloak of protection provided by the Spaniard's armada of duennas reinforced her detachment. In those two years she was a child who had never been a child, living a life of sophistication far beyond her years.

By the time she entered college, the pattern was inherent. Law school, a short stint as mediator, then the sepa-
rateness and secrecy of The Black Watch only com-
pounded old habits. Habits that had become custom. Until
Devlin.

Devlin who barged into her life, smiling his wicked
smile, looking at her tenderly through sad, beautiful eyes.
Devlin, whose absence made her ache with this new and
uncommon loneliness.

Kate wandered the house, dressed in white jeans, a purple shirt, no makeup and no shoes. The hour was late and
the morning spent. Now, the day was bright as it slid into
afternoon. And though she wasn't hungry, or thirsty, the
path of her wandering had taken her to the kitchen. Everything was exactly as she'd left it, except a cup had been
rinsed then set by another on the counter. To await a refill?
With a cup for her?

In her distraction, Kate hadn't given much thought to
the restored electricity. Until now, when both heat and the
scent of coffee wafted from the coffeemaker. Touching a
drop of water clinging to the rim of the cup, drawing upon
pleasant memories, she could see Devlin drinking from it.
His arm flexing, his hand, broad, yet with long, tapered
fingers, circling the cup as he lifted it to his mouth. His
lips touching the smooth edge. His eyes watching her.

Abandoning the thought she feared might lead where
she wasn't ready to go, Kate wandered to the windows.
The tide was high and still angry. Debris from the storm
lay helter-skelter over the shore and the lawn of Sea
Watch.

And he was there, working in the yard.

"Devlin."

As she hadn't admitted she was seeking him, or hoped
he hadn't left Sea Watch, Kate didn't stop to think at all
as she hurried to the deck and down the steps. The pad of

her bare feet masked by the rumbling surf, it wasn't until she touched him, laying her hand on the curve of his shoulder, that he knew she was there.

As he turned, his face was solemn. His piercing look ranged over her as if inspecting for damages. After a time, he laid aside the broken frond he'd taken from a palmetto and stripped off his gloves. Tossing them away, in the same motion he reached for her, drawing her to him, touching his lips to her forehead.

"Morning, darlin'. Or should I say, good afternoon, sleepyhead?" As he held her against his bare chest, his head dipped until his chin rested against her hair. He said nothing else, nor did Kate, as they embraced in the sun.

Beyond the rise and fall of their breathing, neither moved. Until Devlin sighed, and his fingers convulsed, clutching at her shirt. In the manner of a man who feared she would vanish if he let go, he gathered the knitted cloth in his fists.

Pressing her cheek to his chest, listening to the steady beat of his heart, Kate let her hands skim over the corded muscles of his back and shoulders. With her fingers trailing in the wake of her palms, she soothed and quieted a concern she didn't understand. When he gradually relaxed, she stepped away. Not beyond his embrace, but enough to seek an answer for his mood.

When she looked up at him, he touched her face. His gaze followed the path of his thumb as it strayed over her flushed cheek. Something fierce and troubled flickered in his expression as his voice roughened. "I did this?"

Kate couldn't find the right words, the subdued and angry concern in his look swept them away. Turning her face into his hand, she stroked her cheek against his palm. Drawing a breath at last, she answered quietly, "It doesn't hurt." Her voice dropped lower, her hand covered his, keeping it at her face as she looked into his eyes. "Roses in my bed, roses on my cheeks…"

"Don't." Devlin caught her fingers in his as he eased back a step. He didn't want to hear or think about the night. For what he'd been pondering as he worked, and for what he had to say, he needed a cool head. As it was, he'd barely managed to leave her this morning. When he'd wakened, he'd lain by her side remembering. And wanting her again so badly he was in torment.

The only answer for his state was work, grueling and long. At least he'd hoped so. Now he was discovering nothing sufficed. As he looked at her, barefoot and tousled, watching him through heavy-lidded eyes, with the mark of his lovemaking on her, he knew only Kate or distance would be the remedy.

Even as badly as he wanted her, until both had dealt with and resolved some issues, the wisest course was that there be no risk of encounters like the night before.

Distance. He needed to give her that. He needed it as much for himself. And for time to think.

"Kate." Pausing, he looked away. She was too lovely in the sun, with her hair catching the light. Too lovely in a shirt many sizes too large, and nothing underneath. Too lovely with her moist and parted lips swollen from his kisses. "Sweetheart…"

Sweetheart. Somehow the word rankled, when it hadn't before. Perhaps it was his tone. Or that she anticipated what he meant to say. Suddenly the day wasn't so bright, and the scent of roses lingering in her mind grew cloying. Watching him solemnly, with her arms hanging loosely by her side, she bided her time while he searched again for the right words.

"How?" he muttered, "How do I make you understand?"

Kate's mouth went dry. Of all the things she might have

expected, a brush-off wasn't one of them. But that explained his reaction earlier. When he'd embraced her, and clutched at her, he'd seemed to be in distress. And if last night had been a mistake, it would hurt him to say it. She knew him that well, at least.

"You don't have to make me understand anything, Devlin. We made no promises." Kate reached for strengths that had served her all her adult life. Today she found them lacking, but Devlin would never know. "Last night was a pleasant encounter. A product of the heat of the moment. I don't think either of us realized at the time that it would be only a passing fancy, an interlude."

Interlude. The word seemed to haunt her as her tongue almost tripped over it. Reaching deeper into reserves, she continued. "In that, I suppose we misjudged. But that we're here on the island at all is proof we've both been wrong before."

Kate felt the prickle of tears at the backs of her eyes. Tears as much for kind, gallant Devlin as for herself. Tears that hadn't fallen in years, and wouldn't now.

"Devlin." Without thinking she touched his arm, and watched as the color fled from his face. Softly, as if she comforted a child, she said, "You don't owe me anything. You've been a friend. The best in my life. If there's anything to regret about last night, it's losing that.

"I'm sorry, I…" Kate couldn't say any more, the spasm in her throat wouldn't allow it.

With the heat of her touch burning him like a brand, Devlin had forced himself to listen to her pretty speech. A speech meant to let him escape an unspoken commitment he never wanted to escape. Not so long as Kate looked at him as she did now, or wanted him as she had long into the night.

"Are you all through?" The guttural edge in his voice surprised even Devlin. And as Kate's expression went blank, he wished he could soften his tone. But if he did, if he let down his guard at all, she would be in his arms and both of them in her bed before she knew what happened. "I liked your speech, I'm glad I'm your friend, and nothing this side of hell is ever going to change that. Just as nothing is ever going to change last night. It happened, and it was beautiful. Too beautiful not to be honest.

"That's what we need to do, Kate. Be honest. I promised the perfect lovemaking, the wonder for all our lovemaking to follow. I hope it was that. But before we go any deeper into this, we both have issues to resolve, guilt to face and put to rest before we move on.

"You called it the heat of a moment." He looked toward the horizon, and the point where sea and sky blended seamlessly and perfectly into one. As Kate and he. Perfectly. Two blending into one. Turning his gaze back to her, he slid his hand over hers, keeping her clasp at his wrist. "I suppose it was that, and the storm and the rain, and the dark, that made us get ahead of ourselves."

"Ahead of ourselves?" she echoed quietly.

"Yeah, ahead." The trace of his fingers over hers recalled other caresses, and other moments. "Making love last night wasn't a mistake, sweetheart. It was just out of order."

Kate hadn't looked away from him, nor did she now, but her eyes narrowed. Devlin could almost see her lawyer's mind begin to absorb, to analyze, and to speculate on the order of things.

"Ahead of ourselves," she murmured, testing both words and theory, and coming to an understanding. "Because we both have issues to resolve, and guilts to deal with…in order to bring a whole heart into what is between us."

"Is there any other way for us, Kate?" Even knowing that he shouldn't touch her again, that he shouldn't tempt fate, he brushed the curve of her throat and then her lips with his knuckles. Turning his hand, repeating the caress with his fingertips, he watched as her eyes darkened and her lips parted on a softly caught breath.

Steeling himself against the responses he knew he'd deliberately provoked, he asked in quietly thoughtful words, "Would you want less than an unfettered heart?"

Mesmerized by the tone of his voice and by his touch, Kate spoke her denial with only an incalculable shake of her head.

However small, it was not lost on Devlin. Nothing about Kate was lost on Devlin. Driving his point home, he asked gently, "Beyond the heat of a moment, could you give less, my love?"

Kate struggled to be honest and logical. With logic the greatest problem when he was touching her. But when she could think in her best lawyerly manner, she knew Devlin had defined the secret tragedy of Kate Gallagher and Paul Bryce.

Succinctly and gently, with words of wisdom she'd been too blind to see, he'd set her free.

"Give less...?" She began, then knew she hadn't the words for more than the truth. "No." Again that small shake of her head. "Never. In the heat of the moment, or any moment." Not even to Paul.

Especially and never so little to Paul.

Catching the hand that had teased and provoked, she brought it back to her mouth. Over that joined clasp she watched him as her parted lips moved over each fingertip. Fingers, scented pleasantly by leather. Gentle fingers that had known her in sweet, daring intimacy, teaching her much of herself, and more of love.

With her lips stroking each work-worn tip, she remembered their rough caress across her forehead and down her face. Most of all, she remembered their rasping path skimming from her throat, down the slope of her breasts.

"Kate."

In her name, she heard the equal of desire that quickened with her first glimpse of her warm and tender lover. As he worked, his skin marked by the sweat of his labor and glistening in the sun, he was wonderfully, splendidly male. He was power and smoldering sexuality, the primal aphrodisiac that once made no sense to her, drawing her to him. When she touched him and he'd turned to take her in his arms, she knew there could be but one end to this day.

"Kate, no." He saw in her eyes the defeat of his protest.

"Devlin, yes." Though her voice teased, Kate was solemn. She'd misinterpreted in the beginning, then had understood that he meant to suggest a time apart. An interval of reflection and resolution. She needed such a time. So did he. But this day after the storm was too glorious to forfeit to the past.

"There are things I need to say to you." Devlin's face was grim in concentration as she abandoned one focus for another.

Stepping close, lifting both hands to his chest, she let them drift slowly with excruciating care down the lean, muscular lines of his abdomen. Her fingers hovering at the low riding band of his jeans, she tossed back her disheveled mane and rose on tiptoe to stroke his lips with hers. As her breasts grazed his chest, with the flimsy knit of her shirt as nothing between them, she let the tip of her tongue touch the underside of his clenched lips.

But only briefly, for when he sighed heavily and would have reached for her, she danced away. Pausing only a hand's length beyond his reach, she smiled, knowing full well that what her tantalizing had done to her was blatantly visible to the hot, fierce eyes that moved over her in a scorching gaze.

"Kate."

He reached for her again. She danced away again.

"What the…?" Breaking off, raking an agitated hand through his hair, he stared at her. Long, hard, hungry. "What the hell are you doing to me?"

Kate's smile was calm and innocent, but barely hid her delight in this new power. "I was seducing you," she said in a voice that was seduction itself. "Now, having failed in seducing or distracting you, I'm going for a swim. A cold shower sort of swim."

"Kate."

As he called, he snatched at her shirt, but she was too quick for him. Halfway down the boardwalk, she turned. "Kate, Kate, Kate. For such an eloquent man, you *do* sound like a broken record." Backing away, but keeping her gaze locked with his, she called boldly, "You know what your problem is, O'Hara?"

"No, Gallagher, but I'm sure you're going to tell me." She was beautiful there in the sun, teasing and laughing, happier than he'd ever seen her. It might be transient, only the heat of another moment, but if he'd given her this sense of uninhibited joy even for a while, he would cherish it, counting it the gift of fate.

He was smiling as he leaped to the boardwalk. His step was the measured pace of a stalking animal and in his fierce gaze lay challenge. "Well, darlin'? You were going to tell me about my problem."

His prodding question jogged her from a mesmerizing fascination. Remembering the game she played, Kate mustered a saucy grin. "You've been so busy polishing your armor, you don't know a dare, or a proposition, when it's flung at you."

His pace never altered. "You think I don't, huh?"

"Nope." With the rush of the sea at her back, and the sun long past its meridian, Kate watched as he came to her.

He stopped then, hooking his hands in the empty belt loops at the waist of his jeans. The little weight of his hands drew the faded denim dangerously lower. "Wanna bet, lady?"

"Do I wanna bet? Ahh..." Kate began to ease away, making ready for the final challenge. "Yes! I want to bet."

Laughing, Devlin lunged, and this time he caught her shirt. But only because she'd tugged it over her head and thrown it at him. Bringing the purple cloth to his face, he inhaled a clean, irresistible scent of soap and sunlight, and Kate.

She was as naked as he when he caught her. With the surf swirling about them, and the undertow washing sand from beneath their feet, Devlin's kiss was long and deep. When he drew away, taking the hand he offered, she went with him into the sea.

Ardor tamped, but not forgotten, the next hours were spent in quieter water beyond the breaking waves. Sometimes they swam against the tide, and other times drifted with it, catching a wave to the shore. Sometimes they rode the calm surface of deeper waters, hands linked, bodies touching. Other times they dived, skimming the sand, meeting for a kiss or an intimate touch. As they moved together with comfortable ease, if Devlin was more powerful, Kate was most agile, with one a complement to the other.

Once, as they strayed close to shore, a great blue heron stood at the edge of the surf, watching, one leg poised in a half-taken stride, his long neck preening, his black eyes riveted.

"Do you think he's deciding whether or not we're too

much for his dinner?'' Kate quipped as she floated into Devlin's arms.

''Nah.'' His hands cupped her breasts, his mouth nibbled at her ear. ''He's speculating about what a lucky devil I am.''

''Smart bird.'' Laughing, Kate grasped his hair, drawing him down to her salty kiss.

''Jealous bird.'' Devlin countered with a kiss of his own.

The sound of the engine reached them long before the shrimper rounded the curve of the island and set a straight course toward them. By the raucous quarreling of the gulls and the size of the pod of dolphins gliding in its swell, the catch had been good.

''We should go,'' Kate said against his shoulder.

''No. There's something I want you to see.''

''But the crew...'' she protested with belated modesty.

''Let them see.'' Brushing her wet hair from her face, he touched her cheeks. Recognizing that the color in her scraped cheeks was more than a blush. Soon the touch of sun would be more than a touch. ''Let them guess what they want to guess, and know what they want to think they know. Above all, let them envy us.''

Nibbling again at her ear, he whispered, ''Maybe then they'll discover that after a long hard day they aren't too tired to make love to their wives, after all.''

''Devlin!'' The rest of what she might say was lost in the heavy thrum of the shrimp boat.

The engine quieted and slowed. The boat turned a little toward them, setting the water to bobbing and splashing furiously. In the melee, propriety would have been impossible were it not for Devlin's arm placed strategically around her.

''¡Hola!''

The call came from the bow of the boat as it chugged

slowly in a circle rather than its original hell-for-leather course home.

"Hello," Devlin called. "Good catch, I see."

"The best." A loud guffaw followed the cheerful admission. "And you, too, *I* see."

"Yeah!" Devlin agreed. "A mermaid."

"Aye, yi, yi," the captain called. "I'm new to this pretty American coast, I didn't know she had the lovely creatures." Amid cat calls and laughter from the grinning crew that lined the deck, he asked, "What bait did you use to catch this mermaid?"

"My bait? Ah, yes, my bait." Devlin laughed softly. As the water continued to dash and splash, leaving little doubt that both he and Kate were swimming nude, he nuzzled her cheek and kissed her temple. "You tell them, darlin'."

Suddenly Kate saw the humor in their situation. Not caring that these jovial men might see her naked, not caring that they might know beyond any doubt that soon this man who held her would make love to her, she joined in their amusement.

As if her laughter were permission that they might include her in their banter, one of the crew called to her. "*Sí, señorita,* tell us of this bait, so we might catch a mermaid."

From Devlin's sudden wince, the pinch she delivered and its suspected target didn't go unnoticed as she replied sweetly, "His bait? Why, his handsome face, of course."

"Ahh, a mermaid of spirit. You are a fortunate fisherman, sir," the captain called into the roar of more laughter from his crew. As they'd talked, the boat had come full circle. Now, with a touch to the brim of his cap and a smile that wagged his heavy mustache, he set a course for home. "You have made the end of my day a delight. Now I leave one for you. *Adiós, amigos.*"

Gallant that he was, the captain went slowly, the wake

little more than when he circled them. When he was yards away and they were clear of any backwash, he set a speedier course.

Kate watched as the boat moved away, growing smaller. When the sea was quieter, as well, she repeated the captain's promise. "'Now I leave one for you.'" Turning in Devlin's arms, she asked, "What did he mean? What could he leave us?"

With a finger at her lips, Devlin whispered, "Wait, be very still and you'll see."

But when she complied, there was only the quiet sea around them. For the first time that day, time crept by slowly. When she grew restless, sending him a questioning look, he only touched her lips and shook his head again.

Kate was curious, even doubtful, but she did as he asked. With the late afternoon sun slanting down, and with water lapping at her bare breasts, the day was warm and comfortable. Giving herself up to the tranquil rhythm of the tides, she discovered waiting in Devlin's arms could be more than pleasant.

The first subtle touch against her leg startled her, but giving her an encouraging embrace, Devlin reassured her. With the second touch, she understood.

The dolphins that followed the shrimp boat had stayed behind to investigate. Friendly, curious, half-tamed creatures, they swam and dived, and circled. Sometimes they swam at a distance. Sometimes close enough to touch her again. When they perceived these curious, alien creatures meant them no harm and grew braver, Devlin moved apart from Kate.

"Easy, now. Don't make any sudden moves. Just hold out your hand and wait for them to come to you. Let them brush against your fingers, but don't make any overt effort to touch them."

There were three dolphins. Sleek, agile mammals, as

curious as kittens. As playful. As gentle. Kate grew accustomed to the glide of smooth, rubbery skin against her body and her hands. In delight the captain had promised, she watched the graceful swimmers arcing through the long, unhurried curves, taking them down, then bringing them back to the surface regularly for breaths of air.

The smallest was most curious and a clown. His surfacing became more spectacular, with curling leaps and the slap of his tail against the surface of the water. Kate always assumed dolphins were gray, but in this wonderful and amazing proximity, she saw one with a combination of black and white, as well as the expected gray.

After a time, their curiosity sated, the larger dolphin swam away. Eventually, the smaller one followed.

"So," Devlin asked when the water was calm again, "what do you think of our water-bound friends?"

"I think they're wonderful. As you are. Thank you."

"Thank the captain," he demurred. "It was his special gift to my beautiful mermaid."

Circling his neck with her arms, linking her fingers at his nape, she refused his humility. "The gift was yours. From the moment you saw the boat, you planned this. The captain was simply gracious enough to collaborate."

"I didn't plan, my love. One can never plan the actions of wild creatures. But I had hope."

"How did you know?"

"That they might be curious and stay?" A bare, broad shoulder lifted from the water in a dismissing gesture. "I grew up on the Chesapeake, remember?" When he saw from her look the small deprecation wouldn't work, he admitted, "I've worked with dolphins, in a place or two."

Kate was beginning to wonder if there was anything Devlin O'Hara hadn't done. Just as she was beginning to wonder how much of the wandering he admitted to was purely adventure. Kate was certain a heart as kind as his would demand he do more than chase the next thrill. That he must be more than an adventurer.

Since the dolphins left they'd been drifting with the current, which had taken them toward shore. In an unspoken agreement to call an end to the adventure, when they could stand comfortably, Devlin took her hand to walk with her through the surf.

"The little dolphin, was he a baby?" Kate asked.

"Not a baby, but he was young, probably less than two years. I assume he was still with his mother, whose care would have begun with that first nudge to the surface for his first breath."

"How do you know?"

Devlin chuckled. "Not by any great magic. The calves stay with their mothers at least a year, and sometimes two, nursing the whole time. The little fellow looked pretty fat and sassy, so Mama must still be good to him."

The surf was knee-deep, then ankle-deep. With a tug of their clasped hands, Kate drew him to a halt. "Thank you."

"My pleasure."

"How did you know I would enjoy the dolphins so much?"

"A mermaid who studies birds and watches whales." With a lift of a brow, he looked down at her, and when his lips tilted, it was in a smile burnished by the sun. "How could I not?"

"Yes, of course, however could you not?" Kate agreed in a soft voice. He knew, simply because he was Devlin.

When he turned to her, his hands circling her waist, Kate was at ease with his gaze sweeping slowly over her naked body. She welcomed the spark of passion kindling in his eyes. When he brought her back to him, she went eagerly, hungrily.

"Kate, sweet Kate, I didn't mean this to happen. Not

here. Not now," he murmured against her throat. "We have to talk, there are things I must say. Things…"

Kate stopped the flood of words with a touch that brought his lips briefly to hers. Then, moving away a half step for a degree of sanity, she nodded. "Yes, there are so many things. Things we have to resolve. Things we have to say. Even things we must know."

Catching a long slow breath, her voice a whispered plea, she said, "But not when you want me as much as I want you. Not when I want you now, Devlin. Here."

The wordless sound he made as he reached for her was unintelligible. But it said what he'd never put into words. It said all she ever needed to know, as he swept her in his arms to take her to the small gazebo by the boardwalk, where she knew he would make love to her.

What need was there for the words? After all, this was Devlin, who gave her a rose and dolphins to speak his love.

When he stepped within the shade of the quaint and pretty structure meant to give comfort and pleasure to weary beachcombers, Kate wondered how many lovers had loved here, as well. As he let her body glide down his, the hard masculine planes a caress, his gaze keeping hers promised that no matter how many had sought this trysting place, none could ever have loved as Devlin and Kate.

This was *their* moment, their place. Time stopped. There had been no yesterday. There would be no tomorrow. There was only now. Only Kate and Devlin.

No lovers had lain together in the soft shadows. No gentle adventurer had ever drawn his lady down to a lover's bower more beautiful than one of castaway jeans and a purple shirt. And when his body covered hers, seeking entrance, no lover had ever been more needed, more wanted. Never more loved.

When his lips traced the shape of her face, taking the mingled tastes of the salt of the sea and the sweetness of Kate on his tongue, no heart belonged more completely to another.

"Kate," he whispered. Only her name, an endearment none could rival, spoken in a timbre humble and triumphant at once.

"Yes," she answered, though no question had been voiced.

A single word that acknowledged every need and every desire. A word that held the key to Devlin's heart and stirred his passion beyond any he'd ever dreamed.

Barely leashing the rampant hunger that seared his soul, his body embraced and sheathed in her and trembling with the force of his need, he lifted his lips from her kiss. Rising over her, as his bracing arms framed her face and his fingers stroked the wild silk of her hair from her brow, he looked down into the shimmering shades of the golden eyes of a tigress.

This was how she should look. How she would always look in his mind and heart. This was the look of love and desire, of passion and lust. This was the real Kate, lusty, uninhibited, wanton.

This was the look that forever sealed the fate of Devlin O'Hara. The look that swept away control, and decorum, and gentleness. As eyes as blue as a mountain lake darkened to midnight, recalling a memory and a teasing promise made the first night he made love to her, he whispered softly, a warning, a covenant. "This is someday, my beautiful golden eyes."

There in a stranger's borrowed gazebo, on a bed of clothing cast away in haste and with tenderness forgotten, Devlin, the gentle knight who could no longer be gentle, made fiercely passionate love to Kate.

And with the whisper of the sea as their song of love, and the setting sun bathing them in its fiery glow, no mating had ever been so sweet.

Nine

Three days. Devlin wanted three days to deal with the troubles that brought them to Summer Island, and to each other.

Kate had dealt with her own troubles in Devlin's arms. But in the time he'd imposed, she'd done some thinking, better resolving issues from her past. When neither thought nor resolution would've been possible in Devlin's distracting presence.

Smiling, Kate knew she couldn't think of anything but Devlin when he was near. The afternoon of the dolphins and the gazebo proved that. Laughter that had been missing too long from her life rang out over an eerily quiet beach.

"A seductress." Laughter became a musing smile. She wasn't aware she knew how to seduce a lover. But she had. Just as Devlin never intended to make love to her. But he did.

"Wanton." Kate chided herself, with no real shred of remorse. As she remembered untamed lovemaking on the sandy floor of a sunstruck gazebo, she knew that if their roles were reversed, the end would have been the same.

Then the need to deal with separate pasts intruded, and set them apart. But only for three days.

"This is the third." Kate laughed aloud again, and was struck by the commonness of what had once been rare. She'd thought laughter was lost to her, until Devlin. Sobering, she wondered how many times she had said that litany. *Until Devlin.*

How many more times in her life would she say it again?

Countless, without question, for he was responsible for every good thing in her life. The days alone hadn't been bad, because he filled her thoughts. From the moment he'd stepped into her life, Kate Gallagher, ever the loner, was different. Even her hours at the piano had changed. Though she played long into the night, the music was quiet, soothing. Because she was at peace.

The only blot on the days of waiting was a call from Jericho. A call proving her fears.

"Where are you, Tessa?" The soft query was lost in the shivering whisper of palmetto fronds. But Kate was barely aware of the sound or the errant breeze. "What's happened to you?" she wondered. "Why can't anyone find you?"

Mary would have provided for the child, Jericho had reminded her adamantly in the course of their telephone conversation. Yet, in nearly the same breath he'd cautioned her that neither police investigation nor electronic searches had turned up a clue. Despite a state and nationwide search that had come up empty-handed, he kept doggedly to his theory that, given Mary's precarious health, she couldn't have taken the child far. With each day, Jericho became more convinced the child was near. More convinced that time was all that was needed for Tessa to be found.

But, in his thoroughness, he had discovered records of Mary's daughter. An illegitimate child by an unidentified man, a daughter who disappeared without a trace when she was fifteen. But all Jericho learned had happened so many years before the elderly woman had come to Belle Terre.

No one suspected that Mary had any family at all. Neighbors and friends regarded her as a quiet, pleasant woman, painfully alone. When Tessa had appeared, Mary had been evasive, saying only that she was the child of someone caught in a bad marriage.

Both Kate and Jericho strongly suspected there was much more to the truth than the simple excuse. With the discovery of the mysterious, missing daughter, Kate was convinced Tessa was Mary's granddaughter, or even her great-granddaughter. Perhaps the child of a troubled relationship, but of more than friends.

The sudden roar of heavy engines shattered her musing, and the cacophony that marked each hour of the morning began again. It was not so much an unpleasant sound as alien. After spending most of three days listening to the din as it drew nearer, Kate decided she really should have grown accustomed to the snarling machines rather than jumping out of her skin in her distraction.

After the storm, though little of the shell road had washed away, most of what remained was in dire need of repair. In his efficient, concerned manner, McGregor brought his equipment to the island by barge. Under his supervision, his crew began their repairs at the northern-most tip of the island, and moved south. On this the last projected day of work, only a few yards short of Sea Watch, the crew had taken a break for lunch.

For half an hour Kate enjoyed blessed silence. Then came the return of the roar that seemed even louder than before. But it should be brief, for the distance from Sea Watch to the river and a rendezvous with the barge was short. McGregor was as efficient in his work as he was committed to protection of the island.

Soon it would be quiet. And soon Devlin would come.

"Three," he'd said, flashing three fingers. "If you don't come to me, I'll come to you. Three days, Kate." Then again, as if convincing himself it wouldn't be forever, "Only three."

The first passed swiftly, then the second. Wrapped in solitude, she'd done some thinking. And in the private hours, she'd accepted many things.

Now she was eager for Devlin, and the day moved slowly.

The rumbling staccato, broken regularly by the warning shriek of reversing engines coaxed Kate to the railing of the deck. The scene that greeted her was like one from a movie. Brawny men wearing gloves and hard hats moved loads of sand with incredible precision. Monster machines moving in concert across the beach in a ballet choreographed for snarling metal beasts.

Skillfully, to the constant warning beep, men and machine reconstructed the little road. Kate became so fascinated by the orderly chaos the little blond head flashing through patches of sea oats along a dune didn't register.

Catching movement at the edge of her peripheral vision again, she dismissed it as some creature scavenging among the vegetation and settled down to enjoy the spectacle unfolding before her. But her subconscious wouldn't dismiss what it had seen.

Her gaze was drawn from the machines to the dune above them. There was nothing to see. Puzzled, she turned back toward the shore. Her arms resting on the banister, she to tried give her complete attention to the men and the road. But the pull of concern grew stronger. Something wasn't as it should be.

Frowning at a thought that nagged, she straightened and looked to the dune. As she searched past swaying reeds, her frown deepened. Still nothing. No creature prowled. Sea oats stood as unmoving as sentinels. A mistake. An illusion.

"But for a minute I thought..." she began then, breaking off, shook her head. "Of course there's no one there."

Returning to the furor on the beach, her hand reaching for the banister again jerked in midair. *She was there.* Not a scavenging creature on the dune, a little girl on the beach, directly in the path of the packer. A child with blond hair gleaming in the sun as she walked along the newly repaired section of the road of shells.

"Tessa?" As she said the name, Kate knew it was true. As she said the name, the little girl bent to take something from the road. And in the same instant the warning horn screamed reverse.

The operator didn't look back. After all, he'd worked for three days on Summer Island, and the beach was always deserted.

He didn't look back, and the little girl didn't look up.

"Tessa! No!" The words were a whispered prayer and a plea, for no one could hear her call above the din of motors and the warning horn. Kate waited a millisecond, hoping the child would look up and move. In the next millisecond it was Kate who was moving.

Bracing both hands on the banister, she swung over it. The drop to the lawn was more than ten feet but, thanks to Simon, she'd been trained for worse. Landing in a practiced bent-knee roll, she was on her feet and running, her footsteps pounding down the boardwalk. Another leap took her from the landing, over the steps into the sand. Another roll brought her to her feet in a run. Racing past startled men who only had time to turn and stare, she sprinted alongside the packer. She didn't try signaling the operator. There wasn't time.

Even as she prayed for speed and pushed beyond endurance, Kate didn't think she would be in time. But nothing on earth would keep her from trying. A burst of speed she never knew she had took her past the machine. Another sent her dashing headlong in its path. In a step, she scooped the child into her arms, and the great, spinning roller bore down on her.

The blow, when it came, was low and hard. A vise crushed her ribs. Then she was falling, the sickening crunch of shell breaking beneath the packer and the warning horn shrieking in her brain. Before she could scream out her anger at failing, she and the child clutched in her arms were sprawling in scattering, sunlit sand.

It took an instant to realize the machine had roared past them, and another to feel the strong arms that held her. Looking up through a black fog of exhaust smoke, she found blazing blue eyes glaring down at her. "Devlin."

"Are you hurt?" There was anger in his voice and fear. The hands that gripped her were shaking. "Tell me!" he commanded when she was slow to answer. "Are you hurt?"

Then she realized the shore was quiet again. A child who should be sobbing in fear made no sound at all. "No," she said in an unsteady voice, realizing it was because of Devlin she could give that answer. "No, Devlin," she repeated. "I'm not hurt."

"If you aren't, it's not from lack of trying."

Before she could respond to his heated comment, McGregor was there, with his men in tow. "Lord love us! Where in all of this grand earth did she come from?"

He spoke of the child, who clung to Kate, her eyes wide,

tears drying on her cheeks. But still with no sound escaping her tightly drawn and pale lips.

Stress accenting a normally negligible burr, the Scot addressed his fear. "Please tell me the pretty tyke isna hurt."

Brushing tears from a tiny face, Kate made a quick inspection. The small mouth trembled, and golden brown eyes fastened on her. Beyond this strange silence and the frantic clasp at Kate's neck, the child showed no sign of trauma. "She's scared," Kate said, keeping her voice calm. "But I don't think she's hurt."

McGregor leaned over them, his massive, calloused hands reaching out. "Lord love her, give her to me."

The chubby arms about Kate's neck tightened into a stranglehold, the pale face paled more and burrowed into her shoulder. The sob that shuddered through the fragile body was a small note, and still the only sound the child made.

"She's fine where she is," Kate assured McGregor, quickly, forestalling the gruff but kindly man.

Devlin rose from the sand. Reaching down for Kate, he brought them up to him. His scorching gaze stared long at both woman and child, assessing the damage. It was only when he'd seen the truth for himself that he turned to the gathering men. "It's over. No one's hurt," he said quietly in response to mutterings of concern and apology. "We all know no one here is to blame."

"As God is my witness, Mr. O'Hara, I didn't see her." The driver stepped out of the crowd. Faltering, he tapped his hard hat nervously against his thigh. "Maybe I didn't look too good, but we were assured no one but you and Miss Gallagher would be here."

His eyes, green and bright in a weathered face, ranged over the child from blond hair to dainty bare feet. He swallowed, his throat convulsing in unwarranted remorse. "Where the..." Biting back what would likely have been an expletive never meant for little ears, clutching his hat tighter in an iron-handed grip, he asked the question heard over and over, "Where could she have come from?"

Devlin recognized the man who operated the packer. A man of great skills. It was natural he would be most upset. "I don't know."

"Then who does?" The foreman, the biggest of the lot, took a step forward to stand by his crewman. He was massive and burned dark by wind and sun, but eyes like gray smoke were troubled. "She didn't come far. She couldn't, a little thing like that."

"I don't think she came far at all." Devlin stroked golden curls away from a tiny, perspiring nape. Tessa shivered, but didn't cringe away. "With a little investigating, Miss Gallagher, Sheriff Rivers and I should be able to solve the problem."

"Will you let us know?" The big guy again, a ruffian with a tender heart. "I've got a little girl 'bout her size, I wouldn't want this to happen to her. Lost, with big, bad machines nearly running her down."

"As soon as we know anything at all, you'll know," Devlin promised. "But I think that now our best course of action is to get her out of the heat and sun, and to a calmer place."

With Tessa's imminent departure from shore, one by one the crew stepped forward, shaking hands with Devlin, and doffing hard hats in deference to Kate and her daring race against the packer. McGregor was last. Hale and hearty, a man of great deeds and great emotion, he grasped Devlin's hand. "I've never in my life seen anything quite like today. I hope I don't again."

The remnants of the speech of his homeland less apparent in more tranquil times, he leaned close to Devlin, his voice dropping a decibel below the sound of the surf.

"She's quite a woman, lad. If I'm seeing what I think I'm seeing, you're a lucky man."

"Yes, sir," Devlin replied respectfully. "Thank you, sir."

"Ach! I knew it!" McGregor's face crinkled into a broad smile. "I pegged you for a smart man the minute I laid eyes on you. Does my heart good to know I'm right."

Releasing Devlin's hand, with a smile for Kate, the loquacious Scot wheeled about. Crossing the sand in a determined jog, he called out to his crew, "Let's call this a day. Go home, spend time with your families. We'll finish tomorrow."

After the bright autumn heat of the beach, Sea Watch seemed shadowy and cool. When Devlin silently ushered them in, and stepped aside, Kate moved with Tessa to the sofa. Not sure if her legs ached from the leap from the deck, the race down the beach, or the burdened climb back to the house, Kate sank heavily down to the seat.

After a quick look at Devlin confirming that his stern look hadn't altered, she turned her attention to the child. "Tessa."

The child, sitting stiffly erect, didn't move. Beyond the rise and fall of shallow breathing, she was as still as stone.

"Everything's all right, darlin'." Instinctively, without thinking, Kate used Devlin's teasing, soothing endearment. "You're safe now and there's nothing to be afraid of."

There was still no response and no reaction. Not even the rhythm of Tessa's breathing altered.

"No one's mad at you, I promise," Kate whispered, her lips nearly touching the delicate curve of a tiny ear. "Nobody's mad, but I'll bet someone is worrying about you. Maybe even looking for you."

Tessa kept so still, she might easily have been asleep. Or in a fearful trance.

"Please, Tessa." With a puzzled shake of her head, Kate's concerned gaze lifted to meet the hot glare of Devlin's.

But as the turmoil that churned inside him gradually calmed, pieces of confusing and peculiar circumstances began to make sense. As gently as he could, he explained the strange reactions. "Tessa doesn't answer because she can't hear you, Kate."

Kate looked to the child again, wondering if she was injured, after all. The import of Devlin's words hadn't penetrated.

Crossing to kneel before them, Devlin touched a blond curl with a roughened finger. Sweeping it gently from a pale cheek, he tucked it behind her ear. His hand still resting at the hollow at its base, he looked back at Kate. "Tessa can't answer because she doesn't hear you. She doesn't hear you because she's deaf."

"Deaf?" Kate's arms convulsed, bringing the little body close to hers. A frown marked her face. "Tessa's deaf?"

"Yes."

"She didn't hear the warning horn of the packer."

Devlin only shook his head.

"How do you know?" Kate demanded, rejecting what was obvious now. "How can you be so sure? She might have just been too frightened to speak or respond in any way."

Devlin stopped her with a touch. "She wasn't just frightened, Kate. She didn't hear."

The thought of little Tessa with her bright smile and generous nature locked in a silent world was too much. "How?"

"I can't answer that, sweetheart. But I should have recognized the signs sooner." At her questioning look, his lips quirked in a grimace. "More from my Gypsy past, but this time with my family. When I was sixteen, our parents decided it was time we learned the difficulties and appreciated the skills of children with disabilities. As a family we spent a couple of summers working in camps for children with special needs. Some were blind, some deaf, some mentally or physically disabled.''

When she looked at him again with a surprised expression, he only lifted a shoulder in a dismissive gesture. ''No great sacrifice, and not really unusual. It was just something my parents did. The way they taught us.''

Another facet of Devlin's life and Devlin's family. Something to file away for pondering, but in another time. Now she must think of Tessa and Tessa's needs.

And all it seemed the child needed or wanted at the moment was to be held. Perhaps to sleep after the rigors of her journey.

Though he hated to leave them, there were matters to settle. A visit he must make. A suspicion to resolve. Touching Kate's arm, Devlin laid his finger against her lips when she started to respond. With a shake of his head and another touch, this time to the cleft of her breasts, he conveyed that she shouldn't speak because, held so closely, the child would feel the vibration of her words.

''I think she's dozing, or will be soon.''

Kate agreed with a small dip of her head.

''There's something I need to do. Someone I need to visit.'' Devlin stopped short of explanations. There would be time for any number of explanations later. ''You'll be all right while I'm gone.''

It wasn't a question, and Kate didn't answer. But when he tilted her face and their gazes met and held for a long time, she knew the fierceness she'd seen in his eyes was never anger. When he leaned to kiss her, her lips were parted and waiting.

Moving away reluctantly, as he stood, Devlin promised softly, ''I won't be long.''

His gaze moving from Kate to Tessa and back, his look promising more than words could say, he smiled, and turned away.

He was longer than he expected. But not so long he would have anticipated the changes he found on his return to Sea Watch.

The child who had hidden her face in Kate's shoulder sat at a small table with Kate, a cup and saucer before each of them. A bouquet of tattered flowers adorned the center of a pink tablecloth. Flanking the vase was a platter of petite sandwiches and a plate of vanilla wafers.

As he stepped in without knocking, Kate flashed a smile over her shoulder, saying, "Ah, there you are. We've been waiting for you." Touching Tessa's face, drawing her attention to Devlin, Kate said, "We've been waiting for Devlin."

Tessa's gaze lifted from Kate's lips to Devlin. Eyes so uncannily like Kate's they took his breath away, studied him intently, assessing him. He feared she was remembering his stern attitude on the beach. But whatever the child might be thinking, Devlin knew he deserved it. For what seemed forever, he stood, not moving, not speaking, as he waited for Tessa's decision.

When the little girl nodded solemnly, he smiled and moved to the table. Touching Tessa's shoulder, he said slowly, carefully, "My goodness. How did you know I would be hungry for sandwiches and cookies, and thirsty for apple juice?"

Tessa said nothing. Her answer was to pat the empty chair. Once Devlin was seated, in her best tea party manner, she offered sandwiches and cookies for his pleasure. And poured apple juice into a cup once intended for demitasse.

Wondering how Kate had accomplished this miracle,

Devlin took his seat, and having missed breakfast and then lunch, discovered that both the peanut butter sandwiches and the vanilla wafers were delicious. And the apple juice? Today, as he shared this tea party with the two most beautiful ladies he would ever know, it was nectar of the gods.

"That was wonderful, ladies. The best tea party I've ever been invited to," Devlin said at last, patting his flat stomach and smiling for Tessa's benefit. Throughout the game Kate's questioning look had strayed to his time and again. But both knew that, no matter how anxious she was for answers, now wasn't the time.

"Tell you what." Throughout the party, he'd discovered Tessa was a wonder at reading lips. It was Tessa he addressed now. Waiting until she nodded that he should continue, he crouched down beside her. "When I was scavenging in the pantry not so long ago, I found a trunk of toys. If you like to color and draw, there's a stack of tablets and coloring books this high."

With his hands he measured the height, then held up six fingers. "This many. With more crayons and watercolors than you would believe. Would you like me to get them?"

Tessa nodded, then looked quickly to Kate for permission.

"It isn't my house, sweetheart." As Devlin had, Kate knelt, as well, bringing her lips eye level for the little girl. "But I'm sure no one would mind."

Golden brown eyes, fringed by lashes that seemed impossibly long, settled again on Devlin. A decisive chin bobbed again. A hand so soft and chubby and fearless reached out for his.

For the time of a lurching heartbeat, Devlin hesitated, lifting his gaze the little needed to touch Kate's. With the glitter of tears on her lashes, she nodded in answer to his unspoken question. And a smile trembled on her lips as his strong, brown fingers engulfed the short stubby fingers offered in trust.

"Okay." Devlin realized his own smile wasn't quite steady as those tiny fingers lay calmly in his. Rising as Kate did, he added quietly, "I bet that by the time we make our choices, beautiful Miss Kate will have the tea party cleared away, and gorgeous Miss Tessa can draw and color at this table."

Kate could only nod, her heart too full for words. As she watched the gallant, wounded man walk away, the hand of a lost child given without a trace of question into his care, tears she'd fought throughout the little party spilled down her cheeks. When she was alone, she stood listening to their fading footsteps over wood floors, hearing his one-sided conversations that didn't seem so one-sided, after all. When the sound of the pantry door creaking open was followed by Tessa's tinkling laugh and Devlin's deep chuckle, Kate wiped her eyes and turned to clear away their tea party.

"Hobie?" Kate flashed an astonished look at Devlin. "Tessa was staying with him in the gatehouse?"

"It seems Jericho was right all along. Mary did see to Tessa's welfare when she knew she was dying. And, in her condition, she couldn't go far."

"But why Hobie?" Kate's hands were linked firmly in her lap as she watched Tessa choosing another color for her drawing. "With his back, and at his age…"

"He couldn't take proper care of her?"

"No, no." Kate quickly explained, "I didn't mean that at all. But it would have been so difficult." Gripping her hands closer, she said, "It makes sense now…how Tessa seemed to come out of nowhere. When, really she'd just crossed the bridge."

"Still a long walk for one who's only five."

"She's only five?" Tessa was small, but by her manner, Kate had thought she was at least a year or two older.

Devlin frowned, recalling the story Hobie told. "When one lives the life she's lived, it's grow up or else." He stopped short, the alternative was too painful to speak.

"She was abused?" In horror, Kate turned to the child happily drawing houses and stick-figure families.

"Not abused," Devlin explained, keeping his voice low, for he'd discovered that Tessa had a way of divining stress-filled emotions. Acute perception, not hearing. He'd seen it in the camp all those years ago. "Until Mary, not wanted."

"Not wanted? Look at her. How could anyone not want her?"

"I think that's Hobie's story to tell, Kate."

"Where is he now? Why didn't he come back with you?"

"I asked him to wait."

It made no sense to Kate that he would ask that of Hobie. Or that Hobie would agree. "Surely he was frantic about her. Good heavens! Surely he was too concerned to wait."

An expression of bitterness crossed her face as she fell silent, watching Tessa. When she turned to Devlin again, her voice was filled with hurting. "Or doesn't he want her, either?"

Taking her hands in his, Devlin stroked the taut curve of her fingers. "Hobie was concerned and worried half out of his mind. When I arrived at the gatehouse, he'd come back from a search of the riverbank and had just called Jericho."

"Jericho. I didn't even think to call."

"It's all right, love. Jericho's on his way now. Hobie will be with him. He has the missing pieces of this puzzle."

"He told you?"

"Only a little." Releasing her hands, he rose to go to the window. The beach was quiet since McGregor had called a halt to work for the day. Thankful for that thoughtfulness and for the quiet, Devlin said, "He told me only a little, but enough that this begins to make sense. Tessa is Mary's great-grandchild. Her mother was a second generation runaway."

"The daughter of a daughter who disappeared years ago. Long before Mary came to Belle Terre?"

"Yes. Tessa is the daughter of a granddaughter Mary never knew she had. Until she called asking that Mary meet her in Atlanta." Facing Kate again, he gestured toward the shore and the shell road. "Jericho is here with Hobie. The rest of Tessa's story is theirs to tell."

Ten

Hobie stood by the door, turning his hat in his hands, then tapping it against his thigh. An action too recently familiar, recalling the scene on the beach, vividly burned into Kate's mind and memory.

Watching, listening to his faltering greeting, she realized that in all the months she'd lived on Summer Island, she hardly knew him. Until today, he'd only been a smiling face and a friendly voice trapped in an aged, arthritic body.

How many times, in her self-absorption, had she ridden by with barely a wave to him? Yet, how many times had his smile been the brightest part of a particular day? Now, she saw how frail he was and how worried. And she understood that even keeping watch over Summer Island and its tenants must require great effort.

Yet he'd done it. Kate didn't question that it was in that same spirit he accepted the care of Mary's young charge.

Pangs of conscience for her unconcern, and guilt for her

doubt of his devotion to Tessa, plagued Kate. For, if she'd harbored any doubts after Devlin told of Hobie's search of the river, they would have been put to rest the minute she saw his face.

Going to him, with a nod of greeting for Jericho who stood a step behind him, Kate offered her hand. "Thank you for coming Mr...." Pausing, to her horror, she realized she didn't know how to address him, because she didn't know his full name.

But Hobie, being not just a Southern gentleman, but from another, more gallant era, only smiled as his gnarled hand enfolded hers. "A long time ago I was Mister. Complete with a name and even a middle initial." His smile was gently amused as he bowed politely over her hand. "Hobart M. Verey, ma'am, at your service."

He spoke the name with the old and proper pronunciation, giving the last syllable the sound of the letter *a*. Once it had been a proud name, one with much history and a great wealth of land holdings in its estate. A part of which had been Summer Island.

"Now I'm just Hobie, and if anyone remembers, Hobie Veree." This time, giving his name the colloquial pronunciation, in his gentlemanly fashion, he set his hostess at ease.

Kate was surprised there was no bitterness in his words. From the history she'd studied, because the Verey family was also part of the history of Summer Island, she knew the land, wealth, even the good name had been lost by the time Hobart. M. Verey reached adulthood. A financial disaster leaving the following generation, and possibly the last of the line, to live in abject poverty.

But neither the past nor Hobie's gallantry resolved the problem of how she should address him now. A frown drawing her brows down, she said quietly, "I'm sorry, I never knew your name or your connection with the island. All I've ever known to call you…"

"Is Hobie," the elderly man suggested pleasantly, coming kindly to her rescue. "And Hobie's who I am, Miss Gallagher."

"Kate, please." As she said it, she saw that the old man, who had been only a guard to her, had no more patience with even ingrained amenities. "You're anxious to see Tessa, aren't you?" Looking past him to the sheriff, she asked, "You, as well, Jericho?"

Hobie Verey took one small step forward, hat still in hand. "I was wondering where she is. If she's all right?"

"I'm sorry." Kate was shamed by her thoughtlessness. "I should have realized. Expected…"

Devlin's arms circling her comforted her. *"We,"* he emphasized, drawing her back against him. "We should have realized, we should have expected you would be concerned about Tessa and want to see for yourself that she's all right."

"The long walk and the incident on the beach exhausted her," Kate explained. "After the tea party she was so sleepy she could barely hold up her head. She's sleeping soundly and peacefully." With a gesture toward the hall, she offered an invitation. "She's in my bedroom, if you'd like to look in on her."

"I'd like that, Miss Kate." The hat turned in another circle.

"I'll show you the way," she offered.

"No," Hobie said in a voice so low it could barely be heard above the normal sounds of a day that had been anything but normal. "I know the house. I can find her."

Jericho chose to stay behind, but neither of the three spoke as they tracked the sound of his limping footsteps down the hall. When the uneven cadence halted, Devlin was first to comment. "Maybe I shouldn't have asked him to wait to come to Sea Watch until you came, too. But he was so distraught after searching for her for so long, then hearing of the close call on the beach, I thought..."

"You did the right thing." Jericho's interruption was meant to be assuring. Beyond a murmured greeting the formidable and taciturn sheriff had only watched and listened as Hobie said what he had to say. "The day must have been traumatic enough without a frantic relative descending on her. It's good for both of them that she's asleep. Rest for her, a calming time for Hobie."

"How is it that Mary brought Tessa to him?" Kate asked, stepping from Devlin's arms to lead both men to the sofa. "Surely there's a connection, but I can't begin to guess what or how."

"There is." Jericho was no less formidable sitting than standing. His fingers looked too powerful, too intimidating as he plucked a ribbon knotted into a clumsy bow from the table at his side. Letting the yellow satin glide through his fingers to his palms, he folded his fist over it. His dark face was unreadable when he looked up at Devlin and Kate. "A connection I should have found, and would have if I'd been looking in the right place."

The uneven gait signaling the old man's return from the bedroom interrupted Jericho's subdued self-disgust. Almost on cue, each of the three lifted their faces, waiting for Hobie Verey to reappear, wondering if a silent Tessa would be with him.

Meeting their intense gazes, the old man stopped in the doorway. "She's sleeping. Looks like an angel, she does."

Looking from one to the other, he moved his head in a curt nod. "Guess you're wondering how an old, lame security guard came to be guardian of a sleeping beauty?"

Hobie's gaze flickered to Jericho. "Unless you told 'em."

"No, Hobie." The sheriff's stern demeanor didn't alter.

But Kate was learning that it was an expression men like Jericho Rivers and Devlin O'Hara wore when circumstances beyond their control took matters beyond the reach of their protective instincts and skills. Both were inclined to see failure rather than the unpredictable power of fate.

The old man shuffled farther into the room. "You wanted Miss Kate and her gentleman to hear it from me? *It* being a family secret."

"Something like that, Hobie." Jericho's gray eyes never strayed from the guard. That he liked the old fellow was clear. That he was troubled by the situation grew ever more apparent.

"Let me take your hat." Having realized Hobie still clutched his immaculate hat in his hands, Kate stood to take it from him. From long, entrenched custom Devlin and Jericho stood, as well.

Hobie's faded scrutiny followed as she took the hat and crossed to the door and a row of pegs that served as a catch-all in season. He didn't take the chair Kate indicated, until she was seated, flanked again by Devlin and Jericho. Studying one dark-haired man and then the other, he let his gaze settle, finally, on Kate. For a long while he seemed to examine her closely, as if he were seeking something. Assessing.

"I don't suppose it's any wonder that you're all questioning how it came to pass that Tessa's with me." Before his features were almost pained in their worry, now that he'd seen Tessa, Hobie relaxed. "Not a likely choice, an old bummed-up codger like me. Not if there's another choice. Because there wasn't at the time, Mary brought her to me, charging me with a mission.

"So why me? For two reasons. The first was that her only parent died shortly after Tessa came to stay with Mary." The timeworn voice roughened. Hobie coughed and drew a slow breath as his audience waited patiently.

"The second is that I'm the child's only known blood kin."

He waited for the expressions of surprise, and no one disappointed him. "Mary was never legally a Verey, but she could have, should have, been. She was my half sister." Another small cough was followed by another pause. Kate would have gone for water, but an anticipating touch from Devlin stopped her.

"How could it be that she was your half sister?" Jericho asked thoughtfully, but the expression on his face suggested he already knew the answer.

"Mary claimed a lot of names over the years, or so she told me. But the first and true name was Delacroix. I was told she was a beautiful woman." Hobie drifted into the past, then quickly abandoned the memory. "Beautiful like her mother and her mother's mother before her, and destined for the same fate. As was the line that could be traced back far more than a century.

"A family that produced mostly women. All beautiful, each born and trained to be, not a courtesan, but the mistress of one man. These were more than relationships. They were commitments that lasted a lifetime, often spawning second families. As had been the custom for countless years, Mary's mother went on the bidder's block when she was sixteen." Hobie's gaze sought Kate's. "To some it suggests slavery, or prostitution, but it wasn't."

"It was simply a custom of long-standing." Jericho explained an old ritual of Belle Terre. "Mary was in her eighties, so this was only a little past the turn of the century. At that time, many of the ways of the Old South were revered and observed. It doesn't excuse the practice, but men and women held different values then. My own grandfather kept a mistress. It was accepted, even expected among a certain class of Southern males."

Jericho looked to Hobie, at his nod, and to spare him

the breath, he continued, "The women weren't disturbed by the arrangements. They were proud of the price and the stylish lives their exclusive services brought them. If the price was insulting, or the man wasn't acceptable, the girl in question had the right of refusal. Obviously, Mary's mother didn't refuse."

"From the day she was chosen, she lived the life of a queen." Hobie took up the story. "But with little real freedom. Yet she would know that and expect it. The prize of each auction was always the Delacroix woman. They were renown through the South for their spectacular beauty and rare elegance. Mary's mother was the most beautiful of all, and she belonged heart and soul to William Verey, my father."

"Belonged, but never acknowledged," Kate suggested.

Hobie nodded. "Common knowledge, never acknowledged."

"Mary's choice was the same?" Devlin prompted.

"But by then, times were changing." Hobie shrugged a thin shoulder. "People were changing. Not always for the better. Mary went to the bid and the fellow who won her took her away. She was gone for more than sixty years."

"You lost touch?" Jericho, guiding him through the story.

Hobie lifted the bony shoulder again. "You can't lose touch with someone you don't know. She was just a name." He looked up from his gnarled hands, meeting Kate's look. "You might think it strange I didn't know my half sister, but that's just the way it was.

"I grew up on what was left of the plantation. We still had part of the family fortune then, so, as was the custom, my father's mistress lived on a particularly elegant street in Belle Terre. Even today, some of the finest houses are there on Fancy Row. Though a lady of Fancy Row lived well, out of respect for his wife, the Southern gentleman saw to it his second lady and his second family never associated with his legitimate family."

"But his wife knew. You knew," Kate ventured softly.

Hobie nodded. "But neither family suffered for it."

"Mary was the last of a breed, the last of a custom as Belle Terre practiced it. One that deemed you never meet," Devlin mused as softly as Kate had.

"Yes, sir." Hobie agreed. "I never met Mary Delacroix, never knew what happened to her. I never met Mary Sanchez, or knew who she was. Until she came to me about Tessa.

"We were strangers before." The rasping voice was only a whisper. "We were strangers when she died."

"But you took Tessa," Kate said. "Why would you?"

The pride evident in Hobie's gracious manner burned in his eyes. "I took her because she's a Verey. Maybe not by much, but so longs as there's a drop of the blood in her, she's a Verey."

"And because Hobie is Hobart M. Verey, a man of honor," Kate suggested in a thoughtful tone.

"Hobart M. Verey, once last of the line," Devlin added.

Hobie looked at Devlin. "So I believed, until now."

A proud line had dwindled to an old man and one small child with a single name. Tessa.

Kate smiled at Hobie. "There was more Mary asked of you?"

"Two things." His breath stentorious, Hobie was clearly in distress. "That I take her ashes to Wild Wood, the Verey home place she'd never seen. And that I find a home for Tessa."

"The day of the storm." Devlin recalled the unmanned gate, and Kate's concern. "You'd left the gatehouse to fulfill the first promise to Mary. Jericho didn't know her ashes had been claimed, or by whom, because the storm had taken out communications. They were still out when you returned to the gatehouse.''

"Yes, sir. I suppose so. Though I didn't really claim them, not officially. I told some flustered young fellow what I was there for. He showed me to a room, said the urns were labeled and to help myself, then hurried off. I didn't give my name to anyone. Didn't seem right, but it didn't occur to me Sheriff Rivers needed or wanted to know. Not even about Tessa.''

"You had Tessa all along." This from Kate. "She was so close, and we never knew.''

"She saw you, Miss Kate. I think she was coming to find you when she slipped away today." The fire faded from Hobie's eyes. "I didn't dream she would try. In my craziest thoughts, I never would have believed a little thing like Tessa could make the walk over the bridge, then to the far end of the island. When I think of what almost happened…''

"But it didn't." Kate leaned forward to clasp his hand. "Tessa's fine. She was shaken up a bit. But within an hour she was serving a tea party for Devlin and me. And laughing with him while she colored.''

"Tessa laughed?" Nearly colorless eyes sparkled with surprised pleasure.

"Tessa laughed." And so had Devlin. A laugh such as Kate had never heard. Quiet, comfortable, filled with love. She hadn't seen his eyes, but she knew the smile was there, for Tessa.

"I wish I could hear that, Miss Kate.''

"You will, Hobie. I'm sure of it.''

"I don't think so, ma'am. After today, I can see I have to get on with the last part of my promise to Mary.''

"To find a home for Tessa, quickly." Jericho supplied the logical time frame. It didn't require a physician to see what Mary had undoubtedly seen. Hobie's arthritis was the least of his problems. Heart failure was surely a strong trait among the Vereys. The trek along the riverbank hadn't been the best thing for him. But, what else could he do? What would anyone have done?

"The promise that will break what Mary called the Delacroix curse. Women loving men who belonged to other women. Having families that could never bear their rightful name. Until her granddaughter found her, Mary didn't know that for her lost family the path of the Delacroix made them victims of the street, and led to destruction.

"That mustn't be Tessa. Tessa must have an education. Maybe a career. Mary didn't see the girl's hearing as a detriment to anything she wanted to do. *If*," nearly breathless now, Hobie emphasized the word, "*if* she has the right parents."

"Which you must find." Jericho doubted Hobie had the strength to find his way to bed. What did that leave for Tessa?

"Yes, sir." The breaths were quicker, more shallow. "But I think I have already. For now, though, I should go back to the gate."

"What you need is bedrest." Kate wanted to help him.

"Thank you, Miss Kate, but I'm just as well off in the gatehouse. Better, really. I have a lounge chair there that eases me more than lying down."

"Have you seen a doctor, Hobie?" Jericho questioned, the look on his somber face giving way to more than concern.

"Yes, sir, Sheriff Rivers. But there's not much that can be done for a heart that's just plain give up the ghost."

"This has been too much for you. You should rest," Kate insisted, but with a note of pleading.

"I will." He patted the hand she'd laid on his shoulder. "Just as soon as I get Tessa back to the gatehouse."

When Hobie struggled out of the chair, Kate wanted to

help, but turned away, giving him a moment to keep his pride intact.

Then it was the old man who was comforting her. "It will all work out. Don't worry, missy. Most things happen for a reason."

Kate's thoughts were of the child sleeping peacefully in her bed. "Would you mind if Tessa stayed here? Just until she wakes up," she explained quickly. "I could bring her to you then. In the meantime, you could have a while to rest."

"We'll both bring her." Devlin added his assurance.

Hobie's smile blossomed. "I was hoping you would suggest that. Not for me, but so the little one could sleep longer, and wake up in happier surroundings." Going to the door for his hat, with Jericho's hand at his thin arm lending support, Hobie observed quietly, "What could be happier than waking in the house of the lady she came to Summer Island to find?"

"I missed you."

Kate stood at the windows, her back to Devlin, but his words washed over her, sweet and wonderful. Almost as wonderful as his arms circling her, drawing her back to him.

"I missed you." Covering his hands with hers, she murmured, "I missed this. But you were right, we both needed to sort it out, to understand what's between us."

"You said you loved me."

She heard in his voice what he had to hear. Spinning slowly within his embrace, she lifted her hands to his face. "I do love you. I have for a long time. But now, I know that it's right."

"Why did you ever doubt?" Devlin's voice was rough, a little unsteady. "Was it because of Joy?"

"Never Joy." Kate took his hands from her waist. Lifting them to her cheek, then her mouth, tracing the scars on each palm with her lips. Scars that would forever remind her of the battle he waged with Denali for the life of Joy Bohannon and her dream of a child. Closing his fingers over her kiss, she lifted her face to his. "For months I shut myself away from the world, punishing myself with grief and guilt for a man who died at the hand of an assassin whose bullet was meant for me.

"I grieved for Paul Bryce, my partner and my friend. A wonderful man, who told me once, and never again, that he loved me. I wanted to love him. God help me, I tried, but I couldn't. When he stepped in front of me, shielding me from the gunman, I thought I must be some sort of monster. That at least I could have pretended. I could have given him..."

Breaking off, bringing his palms back to her kiss, she whispered, "Then there was Devlin O'Hara, with his crooked, teasing smile. With gifts of morning coffee, a rose and dolphins. Then I finally understood that Paul would have known. The kindest thing I ever did was not to pretend, not to give him half a heart.

"He was too good for half-measures, and deserved more, better. Maybe it would have helped if he'd blamed me, or pressured me. But he didn't. He was just Paul, always there, always kind, always smiling. I know now that he died for his partner, not for the woman he loved."

Devlin wanted to comfort her, but this had to be said. This was the catharsis of strength. Though she didn't understand yet, it was strength that cut her off from the world as she dealt with pain that might destroy her. In time, it was strength that lifted her from the unfeeling limbo. Now it was strength that would lead her to the final healing.

"But when I held him, with his blood spilling over me, I saw love, not forgiveness, in his eyes." Kate had looked away from Devlin, now she met his gaze steadily. "I realize now that Paul never felt there was anything to forgive.''

"Do you know why, Kate?"

Kate smiled, softly, sadly. "Perhaps because he understood better than I that there is no rule that says we must love those who love us, simply because they do. In some strange way, I think he knew better than I that his love was a burden. And I think he hated that."

Her lips tilted as, in recalled tragedy, she found peace. "The last word Paul said to me was partner."

Partner. A single word that spoke volumes to Devlin. In it lay the forgiveness Kate needed months to believe she'd been granted. "He was telling you why he did what he did, that it was about partnership, not love. Paul was absolving you of any blame, sweetheart, because he knew you would have done the same for him."

"I know that now. But I couldn't hear, or understand, the gift he'd given me, until there was you."

"And Tessa," Devlin said quietly.

"Yes." Then Kate's smile was the stunning smile he'd seen that first day in Ravenel's. The smile he had to see again and again. A smile that linked him irrevocably to a beautiful, lost woman, and a special child.

Tessa, who with a simple act of kindness had brought Kate Gallagher and Devlin O'Hara one important step back into the world of caring. Tessa, an innocent child, the sweet-hearted catalyst that led two hurting people to understand the degrees of guilt and love.

Reaching up to him, Kate framed his face with her hands. A face etched with lines that measured his life in smiles. With wondrous eyes just relearning the art. A face she would love all the rest of her life. Rising on tiptoe, she kissed him, her lips saying all that was in her heart.

When she stepped away, Devlin reached for her, his hands spanning her waist. He wanted to make love to her, but now was not the time. Instead he smiled, saying, "You want to go to Tessa, don't you?"

Kate's lashes swept down over her tears for the miracle she saw in his eyes. The love he hadn't spoken, the understanding. When she looked at him again, her gaze was calm and shining. "I'd like to sit with her. She should be waking soon, and I don't want her to be alone and frightened."

"I think Tessa would like waking up to find you by her bed." He touched her cheek with a knuckle, drawing it down to the corner of her mouth before stepping back. The smile was in his eyes when he murmured, "I'll be waiting. For both my girls."

"Hobie seemed better. Stronger." Kate sat on the bench that served as seats in the gazebo. Devlin sat on the floor in the doorway, his head nearly touching her knee, his bare feet resting on the sandy beach.

"Pain and worry can bring the strongest of us down."

Kate watched Devlin sift sand through his hands. Like this, everything he'd said since leaving the gatehouse had been distracted, if not terse. Something was obviously weighing on his mind. Something a long, silent walk on the beach couldn't resolve. Something she knew he would speak of when he was ready.

"Hobie isn't strong in the best of times, Devlin. But, he was glad to see Tessa. When she laughed, I thought he would cry."

Sand drifted through Devlin's fingers and his hand closed into a fist. "Kate, we both know what he's thinking."

"That he's found a home for Tessa with us." Kate wanted to touch him, to stroke his hair, and make him look at her. Instead she folded her hands over her knee. "Except there is no 'us,' is there?"

His fist trembled with the force of his grip. "No."

"Are you saying you don't love me?"

Devlin turned to her. "Is that what you believe?"

Kate's gaze ranged his face, seeing there the truth she'd known in her heart forever. Touching him at last, she stroked his brow as if she would take away his worry. "How could I not believe you love me? The man who gave me the most unforgettable and special gifts of all, honor and peace."

Catching her hand in his, drawing it to his shoulder, he met her gaze steadily. "Now I have to give you the truth."

"About the crash on Denali, and Joy." Intuition, more than a guess.

Devlin didn't speak for a moment. When he did, his voice was ragged. "Joy was already pregnant with the child the doctors said she could risk having."

He hadn't meant to lie. But he had, by omission. Before they could move on together and with Tessa, Kate had to know the death of another weighed on his conscience. She didn't speak for so long, Devlin was afraid and puzzled. "Kate, did you hear me? Because of me a child is…"

"No!" Her palm closed over his mouth, stopping the ugly word. "What you did was what anyone would do. You agreed to take a friend to her husband. If you have to place blame, blame rheumatic fever. Blame Jock Bohannon for choosing to work in such danger. The weather station for not recognizing the storm." Pausing only for a quickly drawn breath before he could interrupt, she said, "Blame Joy. Blame her for putting you in an untenable position. Blame her for not telling you she might not survive the altitude or the cold on Denali, if you should crash. Most of all, blame her for making an ill-advised choice in her excitement."

"Joy wasn't to blame. She couldn't know…"

"Of course, she wasn't to blame," Kate agreed gently

now that her point was made and, she hoped, branded in his mind. "And no, she couldn't know. But, my kind and dearest Devlin, neither could you. That she survived as long as she did was a miracle. A miracle of your making. I've no doubt Jock Bohannon knows and is grateful that you made her last moments as comfortable as you could."

"You believe that?" Devlin had watched and listened, seeing the flame of tigress gold in her eyes as she defended her own. As she defended him.

"With all my heart, as truly as I believe you love me."

"As I love you, huh?" Devlin was grinning. A little wobbly, but still the wicked grin she'd first fallen in love with. "You're sure of that?"

"Beyond a shadow of a doubt."

"I suppose, my love, I should take that to mean you don't need proof."

"Ahh, my beloved knight, I didn't say that." As Kate drew him up to her, with the gleam of desire she knew he couldn't resist, she murmured. "I would never say that."

When his arms close tightly around her, as the fetters of his grief and guilt fell away, in the pounding of his heart against her breast she felt the lifeblood of love.

When he lifted her face to his kiss, in his smiling eyes she saw the joy of love.

When he caressed her, gentle hands seeking, worshiping, pleasuring, his was the touch of love.

When he drew her down with him to a bed of newly discarded clothing, as his body joined hers, in his trembling laughter, she heard a lover's unspoken promise.

And in fulfillment, in that moment of lover's ecstasy, as her heart and body sang with love of its own, she heard him whisper softly, "I love you, Kate. And I always will."

Epilogue

"Sunrise over the Chesapeake."

Standing by the window, admiring the spectacle of dawn over water, Kate loved this moment all the more because it was one of Devlin's favorite memories. Devlin, who laughed and smiled and no longer dreamed of Denali.

Devlin, who made love to her through the night and held her now. Leaning against him, she turned enough to kiss him, before returning to the view. "It's lovely."

"I woke up to this every morning we were here." With his cheek resting against her hair, and his breath warming her skin, he fell silent, watching the fiery ball of the sun lift from the sea.

"It's different all over the world, but no matter where it is, seeing the sun rise makes one believe in miracles," Kate said.

"You're thinking of Tessa, hoping she might hear again."

In the year since the last O'Hara reunion, much had happened. Kate and Devlin had married, in a joyous ceremony surrounded by all the O'Haras. Through the adoption proceedings, with Simon's help, they'd discovered Tessa truly had no other relatives. But the best discovery was that she hadn't been born deaf, or so silent, and it was possible she might hear again. They'd been offered small hope. But any hope at all was a godsend.

"What will you do, sweetheart, if the doctors Simon and my father bring in say there's no help for her?"

"I'll be sorry. I'll probably cry a little, but it won't change my determination to give Tessa every opportunity. Her lack of hearing might be a nuisance, but never a handicap."

Devlin chuckled. "He did a good job."

Turning in his arms, Kate looked up into a face that had grown more handsome in peace and happiness. "He?"

"Hobie," Devlin responded. "He did a good job when he chose you for Tessa's new mother."

"He didn't do so badly when he picked you for her father."

"You think so, Mrs. O'Hara?"

"I do indeed."

"But you didn't have anything to do with the choice?"

Kate had slid into a robe when she left the bed. Devlin was demonstrating how adept he'd become at untying silken knots. As he slipped his hands beneath the open lapels, Kate gasped at his touch, but managed to cling to one more minute of sanity. "What I truly think is that Tessa led us all to the right choices."

"And I'm the right choice for Kate Gallagher."

"Ahh, yes."

"Show me."

Much later, Kate rose over Devlin. Looking down at him, saying nothing, as a slow frown formed on her features.

Though tensions that once ruled her life were long in the past, as he brushed her hair from her face, Devlin asked in quiet concern, "Something wrong, love?"

"I was just thinking."

"Sounds serious. Looks serious. Tell me."

"I was wondering what would have happened to us if you hadn't come to Summer Island. If we hadn't met."

"But we did meet. On one of the best days of my life."

"We owe all this to Valentina."

"My nosy, bossy, meddling sister?"

"Your wise and wonderful sister."

Devlin laughed. "Don't forget Simon's fine hand in this. I'm beginning to think he's a closet cupid."

"He's also a pushover for little girls. Have you noticed he's fallen in love with Tessa? They look so funny together on the beach. Gruff, tough Simon, who never bends an inch, at Tessa's beck and call as she dances around his feet." Kate laughed at a memory. "Did you know he let her bury him in the sand yesterday? Patience's boys helped, but it was Tessa who persuaded him."

"Persuaded?" Devlin lifted a doubting brow, for he'd seen what a sucker Simon was for Tessa. "She had to persuade?"

"Okay," Kate amended. "Tessa asked."

"With no more signing on Tessa's part than the batting of those great brown eyes, I'd bet." Devlin had only chuckled before, now he laughed for real. "Wouldn't the leaders of the world and his enemies in our own government love to see Simon, the fearless Scot, buried up to his neck in sand. With two dark-haired warriors and one tow-headed Indian maiden doing a war dance around him."

"But we'll never tell, will we?"

"Nah." Drawing her down to him, Devlin kissed her

and tucked her head on his shoulder. "You're happy here, aren't you?"

"I love your family. They're wonderful, and what I dreamed of and longed for when I was a girl. So, of course, I'm happy here. But as perfect as this is, I'd be happy anywhere with you."

"But?"

Growing more certain each day that Devlin could read her mind, Kate broached a concern. "Do you think Hobie would ever consider coming to live with us?"

"So that's what's been bothering you."

"Not bothering, concerning." Idly she stroked his chest and kissed his throat. "He's alone, and not well. And, yes, I do worry."

"Hey, is this what my life is going to be like...you filling the house with strays?"

A sharp slap against his abdomen drew a groan and a laugh as she scolded him. "Hobie isn't a stray, and this is serious."

"I know, sweetheart. I know. But you do understand, don't you, that Hobie will never leave Summer Island."

Kate shook her head, letting her hair drift slowly across his chest. "I suppose I should. But he needs someone, even if he won't admit it."

"Yes, he does," Devlin agreed. "That's why I made an offer on the Sea Watch. An offer the owner accepted. It's a done deal, darlin', contingent on your approval, of course."

Kate had been moving over him, evincing her own particular sort of sweet torture. Now she was still, staring down at him. "You would buy the Sea Watch?"

"If it's what you want. I know you love the house and the island. And there's Hobie and Tessa to consider."

"You would settle down?"

"It's part of the marriage deal, remember? Home, family. Daddy spoiling his girls. Making babies."

"What would you do?" Now it was Kate who laughed. "Besides that, I mean."

"There's a good college in Belle Terre. I was thinking we could both take some courses. Work toward helping Tessa and children like her."

"You would do that?"

"If I'm going to settle down, I might as well make it count." Wrapping his arms around her, drawing her closer, he said, "In the bargain, we'd solve the problem of Hobie. We'd be close if he needed us, and he could see Tessa anytime he wanted. So, darlin', what do you think?"

"I think I love you more than I knew." Kate folded her hands over his chest and propped her chin nearly against his. "About those babies. I think I'd like a boy exactly like his father, now."

"Now?"

"Is there a better time?"

"None that I can think of, darlin'. None at all."

In laughter two healed souls reached out to each other and the future. With peaceful minds, they loved as they knew they were meant to love. With whole hearts, and no regrets.

*   *   *   *   *

Look Who's Celebrating Our 20th Anniversary:

Celebrate 20 YEARS

"Silhouette Desire is the purest form of contemporary romance."
—*New York Times* bestselling author
Elizabeth Lowell

"Let's raise a glass to Silhouette and all the great books and talented authors they've introduced over the past twenty years. May the *next* twenty be just as exciting and just as innovative!"
—*New York Times* bestselling author
Linda Lael Miller

"You've given us a sounding board, a place where, as readers, we can be entertained, and as writers, an opportunity to share our stories.... You deserve a special round of applause on...your twentieth birthday. Here's wishing you many, many more."
—International bestselling author
Annette Broadrick

Silhouette Desire

SILHOUETTE'S 20ᵀᴴ ANNIVERSARY CONTEST
OFFICIAL RULES
NO PURCHASE NECESSARY TO ENTER

1. To enter, follow directions published in the offer to which you are responding. Contest begins 1/1/00 and ends on 8/24/00 (the "Promotion Period"). Method of entry may vary. Mailed entries must be postmarked by 8/24/00, and received by 8/31/00.

2. During the Promotion Period, the Contest may be presented via the Internet. Entry via the Internet may be restricted to residents of certain geographic areas that are disclosed on the Web site. To enter via the Internet, if you are a resident of a geographic area in which Internet entry is permissible, follow the directions displayed on-line, including typing your essay of 100 words or fewer telling us "Where In The World Your Love Will Come Alive." On-line entries must be received by 11:59 p.m. Eastern Standard time on 8/24/00. Limit one e-mail entry per person, household and e-mail address per day, per presentation. If you are a resident of a geographic area in which entry via the Internet is permissible, you may, in lieu of submitting an entry on-line, enter by mail, by hand-printing your name, address, telephone number and contest number/name on an 8"x 11" plain piece of paper and telling us in 100 words or fewer "Where In The World Your Love Will Come Alive," and mailing via first-class mail to: Silhouette 20ᵗʰ Anniversary Contest, (in the U.S.) P.O. Box 9069, Buffalo, NY 14269-9069; (In Canada) P.O. Box 637, Fort Erie, Ontario, Canada L2A 5X3. Limit one 8"x 11" mailed entry per person, household and e-mail address per day. <u>On-line and/or 8"x 11" mailed entries received from persons residing in geographic areas in which Internet entry is not permissible will be disqualified.</u> No liability is assumed for lost, late, incomplete, inaccurate, nondelivered or misdirected mail, or misdirected e-mail, for technical, hardware or software failures of any kind, lost or unavailable network connection, or failed, incomplete, garbled or delayed computer transmission or any human error which may occur in the receipt or processing of the entries in the contest.

3. Essays will be judged by a panel of members of the Silhouette editorial and marketing staff based on the following criteria:

> Sincerity (believability, credibility)—50%
> Originality (freshness, creativity)—30%
> Aptness (appropriateness to contest ideas)—20%

Purchase or acceptance of a product offer does not improve your chances of winning. In the event of a tie, duplicate prizes will be awarded.

4. All entries become the property of Harlequin Enterprises Ltd., and will not be returned. Winner will be determined no later than 10/31/00 and will be notified by mail. Grand Prize winner will be required to sign and return Affidavit of Eligibility within 15 days of receipt of notification. Noncompliance within the time period may result in disqualification and an alternative winner may be selected. All municipal, provincial, federal, state and local laws and regulations apply. Contest open only to residents of the U.S. and Canada who are 18 years of age or older, and is void wherever prohibited by law. Internet entry is restricted solely to residents of those geographical areas in which Internet entry is permissible. Employees of Torstar Corp., their affiliates, agents and members of their immediate families are not eligible. Taxes on the prizes are the sole responsibility of winners. Entry and acceptance of any prize offered constitutes permission to use winner's name, photograph or other likeness for the purposes of advertising, trade and promotion on behalf of Torstar Corp. without further compensation to the winner, unless prohibited by law. Torstar Corp and D.L. Blair, Inc., their parents, affiliates and subsidiaries, are not responsible for errors in printing or electronic presentation of contest or entries. In the event of printing or other errors which may result in unintended prize values or duplication of prizes, all affected contest materials or entries shall be null and void. If for any reason the Internet portion of the contest is not capable of running as planned, including infection by computer virus, bugs, tampering, unauthorized intervention, fraud, technical failures, or any other causes beyond the control of Torstar Corp. which corrupt or affect the administration, secrecy, fairness, integrity or proper conduct of the contest, Torstar Corp. reserves the right, at its sole discretion, to disqualify any individual who tampers with the entry process and to cancel, terminate, modify or suspend the contest or the Internet portion thereof. In the event of a dispute regarding an on-line entry, the entry will be deemed submitted by the authorized holder of the e-mail account submitted at the time of entry. Authorized account holder is defined as the natural person who is assigned to an e-mail address by an Internet access provider, on-line service provider or other organization that is responsible for arranging e-mail address for the domain associated with the submitted e-mail address.

5. Prizes: Grand Prize—a $10,000 vacation to anywhere in the world. Travelers (at least one must be 18 years of age or older) or parent or guardian if one traveler is a minor, must sign and return a Release of Liability prior to departure. Travel must be completed by December 31, 2001, and is subject to space and accommodations availability. Two hundred (200) Second Prizes—a two-book limited edition autographed collector set from one of the Silhouette Anniversary authors: Nora Roberts, Diana Palmer, Linda Howard or Annette Broadrick (value $10.00 each set). All prizes are valued in U.S. dollars.

6. For a list of winners (available after 10/31/00), send a self-addressed, stamped envelope to: Harlequin Silhouette 20ᵗʰ Anniversary Winners, P.O. Box 4200, Blair, NE 68009-4200.

Contest sponsored by Torstar Corp., P.O. Box 9042, Buffalo, NY 14269-9042.

ENTER FOR A CHANCE TO WIN*

Silhouette's 20th Anniversary Contest

Tell Us Where in the World You Would Like *Your* Love To Come Alive... And We'll Send the Lucky Winner There!

Silhouette wants to take you wherever your happy ending can come true.

Here's how to enter: Tell us, in 100 words or less, where you want to go to make your love come alive!

In addition to the grand prize, there will be 200 runner-up prizes, collector's-edition book sets autographed by one of the Silhouette anniversary authors: **Nora Roberts, Diana Palmer, Linda Howard** or **Annette Broadrick**.

DON'T MISS YOUR CHANCE TO WIN! ENTER NOW! No Purchase Necessary

Where love comes alive™

Visit Silhouette at www.eHarlequin.com to enter, starting this summer.

Name:

Address:

City: State/Province:

Zip/Postal Code:

Mail to Harlequin Books: **In the U.S.**: P.O. Box 9069, Buffalo, NY 14269-9069; **In Canada**: P.O. Box 637, Fort Erie, Ontario, L4A 5X3

*No purchase necessary—for contest details send a self-addressed stamped envelope to: Silhouette's 20th Anniversary Contest, P.O. Box 9069, Buffalo, NY, 14269-9069 (include contest name on self-addressed envelope). Residents of Washington and Vermont may omit postage. Open to Cdn. (excluding Quebec) and U.S. residents who are 18 or over. Void where prohibited. Contest ends August 31, 2000.   PS20CON_R2